LONDON'S MOST DESIRABLE DOCS

Heroes, heartbreakers…and husbands?

Amongst the glittering lights of London the hard-working doctors and nurses at The Royal are the talk of the town—and none more so than Hugh and Anton!

Passionate and dedicated, these brilliant docs spend all day saving lives and all night breaking hearts. Their own hearts are kept under lock and key…until two sexy single ladies turn their lives upside-down and force them to question everything they ever believed in!

Don't miss the
London's Most Desirable Docs duet
by Carol Marinelli

PLAYING THE PLAYBOY'S SWEETHEART

and

UNWRAPPING HER ITALIAN DOC

Both titles are available now!

Dear Reader

I have especially enjoyed writing these two stories, because the first is set in summer and it's rather lovely to watch as Emily's little holiday break becomes rather more complicated—thanks to the very charming, very blond Hugh.

Then I got to take myself straight into winter and a lovely English Christmas, with Louise determined to enjoy it this year. She's rather cheeky, *very* flirty, and absolutely the last thing that brooding, incredibly sexy Anton needs right now.

Ho, ho, ho!

And in the midst of all that along came Alex and Jennifer, tap-dancing across the stage as I tried to write—more about them later!

I love my job!

Happy reading

Carol x

PLAYING THE PLAYBOY'S SWEETHEART

BY
CAROL MARINELLI

First published in Great Britain 2014
by Mills & Boon, an imprint of Harlequin (UK) Limited,
Large Print edition 2015
Eton House, 18-24 Paradise Road,
Richmond, Surrey, TW9 1SR

© 2014 Carol Marinelli

ISBN: 978-0-263-25474-7

Printed and bound in Great Britain
by CPI Antony Rowe, Chippenham, Wiltshire

Carol Marinelli recently filled in a form where she was asked for her job title and was thrilled, after all these years, to be able to put down her answer as 'writer'. Then it asked what Carol did for relaxation. After chewing her pen for a moment Carol put down the truth—'writing'. The third question asked: 'What are your hobbies?' Well, not wanting to look obsessed or, worse still, boring, she crossed the fingers on her free hand and answered 'swimming and tennis'. But, given that the chlorine in the pool does terrible things to her highlights, and the closest she's got to a tennis racket in the last couple of years is watching the Australian Open, I'm sure you can guess the real answer!

Recent titles by Carol Marinelli:

200 HARLEY STREET: SURGEON IN A TUX◊
TEMPTED BY DR MORALES†
THE ACCIDENTAL ROMEO†
SECRETS OF A CAREER GIRL~
DR DARK AND FAR TOO DELICIOUS~
NYC ANGELS: REDEEMING THE PLAYBOY**
SYDNEY HARBOUR HOSPITAL:
   AVA'S RE-AWAKENING*
HERS FOR ONE NIGHT ONLY?
CORT MASON—DR DELECTABLE
HER LITTLE SECRET
ST PIRAN'S: RESCUING PREGNANT CINDERELLA+

◊*200 Harley Street*
†*Bayside Hospital Heartbreakers!*
***NYC Angels*
**Sydney Harbour Hospital*
+*St Piran's Hospital*
~*Secrets on the Emergency Wing*

**These books are also available in eBook format
from www.millsandboon.co.uk**

**Praise for
Carol Marinelli:**

'A compelling, sensual, sexy,
emotionally packed, drama-filled read
that will leave you begging for more!'
—*Contemporary Romance Reviews* on
NYC ANGELS: REDEEMING THE PLAYBOY

PROLOGUE

HUGH LINTON CAME with a warning attached.

Emily hadn't even put on her scrubs for her first shift as theatre nurse at The Royal—a busy London hospital—before being told by Louise, one of the other nurses, that the surgical registrar who was operating this Monday morning was, by anyone's standards, a heartbreaker.

'Is Candy very upset?' Louise asked a colleague as she tucked her long blonde hair into her hat.

'What do you think?' came the response. 'I just saw her in the canteen, crying her eyes out with a little crowd gathered!' She smiled at Emily. 'I'm Annie.'

'Hi, Annie,' Emily said, but Annie was already back talking to Louise.

'Mind you,' Annie continued, 'I don't get why she's carrying on so much—surely everyone should know that if you go into any sort of a relationship with Hugh it's going to be fleeting at best, heartbreak at worst.'

'Watch yourself.' Louise winked at Emily.

'No need to,' Emily said, 'because he shan't be breaking mine!' But though she had laughed as she'd said it, in fact she wasn't joking.

Emily loathed anything remotely fleeting and no one would get close enough to break her heart. She had decided that many, many years ago.

Still, she was somewhat sideswiped by Hugh Linton's exceedingly good looks because when he first walked into the operating theatre Emily found out first-hand what the word 'presence' meant.

He was very tall and his hair was as blond as Emily's was dark. He had the greenest eyes that she had ever seen and his voice was deep and clear, the type who rarely needed to repeat themselves. His smile, as he chatted with Louise and then caught Emily's eye, did make a slight blush spread across Emily's cheeks and confirmed what she already knew—Hugh Linton was *far* from her ideal man!

'Morning, everyone!' Alex, the senior consultant, came in, having just been in to have a last word with the patient before surgery. 'It's going to be a long one,' he warned as he went off to scrub.

The operation was for the removal of an abdominal tumour in a twenty-six-year-old man. It was a complex tumour and before the operation commenced and the patient was brought in, Alex explained why he was doing open surgery as opposed to keyhole, which was his speciality. Then there was time for a little chat.

'I've already heard about your weekend, Hugh,' Alex said, as he was helped into his gown and gloves. 'I've heard about it from several sources, in fact, and so I don't need to hear it again.'

Hugh just grinned.

All joking was cast aside, however, when the patient was opened up and the tumour was found to be worse than Alex had been expecting.

Emily was, this morning, the circulation nurse, a part of which meant ensuring the operating field was uncontaminated as well as accounting for equipment. Emily loved most roles in Theatre but circulation or scrub nurse were her two favourites and today it was nice to watch how the surgeons worked from a distance, so she could know their nuances when she scrubbed in.

'Not good,' Alex said, once he had opened the patient and taken a good look around. 'We're going to be here for a few hours, Rory,' he said to the anaesthetist.

It was a very long and intricate operation but it went very smoothly, even with a difficult turn of events—though not for the patient. Instead, there was unexpected news for the chief surgeon.

'Alex, Jennifer is on the phone,' Louise said, and Emily watched as Alex paused and frowned.

'Bring the phone over to me.'

Louise held the phone to Alex's ear and Emily glanced over at Hugh, who was looking at his boss as he spoke to his wife—she had clearly asked not to be put through.

'Well, they're under my instructions to put you through if you call,' Alex said, and then listened for a moment. 'I'm here for a couple more hours at least,' Alex said, and then listened some more. 'Okay, darling, please keep me informed. I love you.'

When Louise turned off the phone Alex was quiet for a moment before revealing his news. 'Jennifer's up on the delivery ward.'

'When is she due?' Hugh asked.

'Not for another six weeks.' He carried on working. 'How long do fourth babies take, Louise?' he tossed out to the runner. 'Small ones?'

'Hopefully more than two hours.' Louise answered his black humour with her own. 'I'm a midwife as well,' she explained to Emily.

Theatre was an intricate and complicated world.

Every swab was counted, every pause noted, every instrument's date of sterilisation checked, not a single blade or needle went unnoted—a seemingly seamless task but it was the black box of surgery and one that required a whole lot of effort from the first to the last in the room.

A small pause in proceedings ensued as Alex and Hugh had a drink of water and then re-gloved then they got back to work and Alex somehow did what he had to and concentrated on the patient.

There was no rushing.

For the young man on the table Alex Had-field's work was his very best chance at life. Emily watched as Alex explained things to Hugh and carried on as if his wife wasn't in premature labour halfway down the corridor, but close to midday he looked over at Hugh.

'I can take it from here,' Hugh said, as Louise took a phone call.

'I have your wife on the phone,' Louise said, and Alex pulled of his gloves and took the phone and told Jennifer that he was on his way.

'Oi,' called Hugh as Alex walked off. 'Don't we get to know?'

But Alex was gone.

Hugh asked for a swab count before he closed, as was procedure.

Then he asked for another one.

Emily took no offence.

The operation had been interrupted, and she was also new.

Emily took absolutely no offence and counted again all the swabs and the instruments carefully.

It was her job to do so.

'Thanks,' Hugh said as, satisfied nothing was amiss, he started to close.

Lunch was *very* welcome but Emily found herself concentrating on more than her food when Hugh took a seat near her.

He smelt fantastic—somehow crisp even after hours spent operating—and his long outstretched legs were far too easy on the eye.

Oh, he was so far from ideal!

Emily's ideal man came with some very specific prerequisites—looks didn't matter, she would prefer that he was serious and that he didn't make her laugh too much.

Neither must Emily's perfect man imbue in her a sudden desire to get naked.

No, Emily's perfect man was perfectly nice if somewhat staid.

In her ideal world they would have sex on Saturdays, more out of obligation than necessity—occasionally on Tuesday if Emily was on a late shift the next day and there was nothing good on television.

'You're new?' Hugh said.

'Emily has been working here for a year now!' Louise, the nurse who had warned Emily about him in the changing room, quipped. 'How rude that you haven't noticed her before.'

It was just a small exchange, a teeny bit of fun, but Emily felt a slight flutter of unease as his green eyes told her that he certainly had noticed!

'Emily Jackson,' she said.

Hugh certainly had noticed her—from her pale blue eyes to her creamy skin. He wanted to know if the dark curl that peeked from beneath her theatre hat came from long or short hair and Emily's soft Scottish accent also had him curious.

'How long have you been in London?' Hugh asked. 'It can be a bit daunting at first.' He was about to suggest that he could show her around perhaps when she interrupted him with a slightly wry smile.

'I guess it was at first but I've been living here for years now, so I'm completely undaunted.'

She had meant to shut him down but Hugh had merely smiled. 'Really?'

Let the flirting begin, his eyes said.

Except Emily refused to go there.

Quite simply, *he* daunted her.

Hugh took a phone call and his face broke into a smile. He offered his congratulations and then told everyone the good news. 'It's a little girl and her name is Josie and she's doing very well.'

'How much did she weigh?' Louise asked.

'I forgot to ask,' Hugh admitted, and then stood. 'I'd better go—a hernia repair awaits me.' He turned and smiled at Emily. 'It was nice to meet you.'

'Same,' Emily said, and she smiled but, and Hugh couldn't quite get it, there was something about her smile that he could not put his finger on. It was pleasant, friendly even and yet…he could not find the word.

The afternoon list flew by and Hugh was just about to head up to the wards to check on his postoperative patients when he found out about the hair beneath her theatre cap.

Emily's hair was long, thick, dark and curly. Without the shapeless theatre scrubs Hugh also noticed a curvy figure dressed in jeans, a heavy jacket and long boots.

'See you,' Hugh said.

'Have a good night.' There was that smile again and Hugh found the word he was looking for.

Sparing.

It was an incredibly cost-effective smile—it did its job but no more than that.

Already he wanted more.

No doubt Emily had been warned about him,

Hugh reasoned, because he had felt the coolness of her brush-off. Or perhaps she was already involved with someone?

Still, even with Emily's best efforts to deny that he moved her, the sparks flew between them whenever they were in Theatre together. So much so that at a Christmas work party a few weeks later Emily was relieved when Gina, an anaesthetist, offered her a lift back to her flat from the party, though she warned Emily that she was leaving in fifteen minutes.

With that deadline in mind, knowing she had a legitimate reason to leave soon, when Hugh offered to get Emily a drink she didn't refuse.

'Just a small one,' Emily said, handing him her glass. 'I'm going soon and I don't want to miss my lift.'

Hugh returned with her drink a short while later and an offer too. 'I can give you a lift if you want to stay a bit longer.'

Emily shook her head. 'I have to be up early— I'm going up to Scotland tomorrow.'

'Have you got family there?'

'My mum.' Emily nodded. 'And quite a bit of extended family too.'

'Do you have family here in London?'

Emily nodded again. 'When my parents broke up my dad moved to England...' Emily hesitated; she didn't want to remember that time, moving in with dad's girlfriend Katrina and her daughter Jessica. It actually hurt to recall those events so she hurriedly glossed over them. 'I used to come down a lot to visit.'

'How much?'

'Half the school holidays, but when I left school I moved permanently down here to do nursing.'

'I see.'

'You don't!' Emily rolled her eyes. 'Honestly, we'd be here till next week if I tried to explain it.'

'I'm fine with that.'

There was a sudden plummet in Emily's stomach as they moved deeper into conversation; she looked into very green eyes that, though smiling, for Emily spelt danger.

'So,' Hugh asked, 'will you be in Scotland for Christmas?'

'No.' Emily shook her head. 'I'm working, new girl and all that.'

She chose not to tell him that she preferred to work at Christmas. It was always a painful time. Whether she spent it at her mother's or father's, Emily always felt like a bit of a spare wheel. Her mum and second husband doted on Abby, their daughter together. As for her dad, he was now married to his latest—Donna—and was a father to one-year-old twins.

Yes, it was far too complicated to explain it all to Hugh.

'So what are you doing for Christmas?' Emily asked instead.

'I'll be at my parents',' Hugh said. 'My sister has just had a baby, first grandchild...' He gave a teeny eye-roll. 'I'm to be on my best behaviour and not upset Kate.'

'Your sister?'

'Yep,' Hugh said.

'You don't get on?'

'We do get on,' Hugh corrected, 'usually.'

He was the easiest person she had ever spoken to and for Hugh it was the same. He had tried to talk to Alex yesterday about his sister Kate and had asked how Jennifer was doing, given that their babies had been born around the same time. Hugh had been told that Jennifer was coping beautifully, despite Josie being her fourth and prem.

Hugh had said nothing then about his concerns for his sister, though he voiced them easily now.

'I think she's got postnatal depression.' Hugh said to Emily what he hadn't to his boss. 'But I have no idea apparently.' Hugh sighed. 'At least, according to my mother, my father, my brother-in-law, oh, and Kate too.'

'It's difficult,' Emily said. 'I remember when Donna had the twins…' She faltered and Hugh noticed.

'Donna?'

'My dad's second wife.'

She had tried so hard not to go there but now

that she had she told him a bit more. 'When they were born I had to help out a lot. I was ever so worried.' She thought for a moment about Hugh's situation. 'Can you try talking to her husband again?'

'I might.' Hugh nodded. 'What did your dad do?'

'Not much.' Emily gave a tight smile. She could hardly tell Hugh she had been worried that if things didn't improve, and quickly, that her dad would have been out of the door.

'So, what did you do?'

'I took her to see her GP,' Emily said. 'I rang them and explained my concerns and then made the appointment for her and took her. Things did pick up. It took a while, but they did.'

Yes, things had picked up. Emily had done everything she could to not fall in love with her two half-brothers, but getting up at night, bathing them, feeding them, of course she had.

'How is she now?'

Emily chose not to answer.

'I'd better go.'

'Emily?'

She didn't want to answer, she didn't want to say that, yes, while Donna was fine now, she wasn't so sure that the marriage was.

'Stay for a bit longer,' Hugh pushed.

She didn't want to, though, because she opened up too easily to him.

Fleeting.

She recalled Annie's words.

Heartbreak.

Neither of those did she need.

She wanted her perfect man—one that meant she could hold onto her heart.

Right now that heart was hammering in her chest and very possibly about to be set free if that lovely, sexy mouth moved just a few inches closer, which it was possibly about to do.

'I really do have to go…' Emily chose to play it safe.

'Why?'

'I told you—I don't want to miss my lift.'

'And I told you—I'm very happy to drive you home.'

Hugh had more than noticed Emily and had hoped to get to know her some more tonight.

In the weeks she had been at The Royal she had intrigued him—Emily was friendly yet distant at the same time, and not just with him. Yes, she chatted easily with her colleagues and there was no doubt she was an extremely efficient nurse yet, and Hugh couldn't quite put his finger on it, she held back, really revealing nothing.

Until tonight.

That small sliver of information about her parents had Hugh wanting to know more about Emily.

She was a curious girl, Hugh thought.

Something told him there was a lot more going on in that sensible head of hers and her cool exterior told Hugh that the full force of his charm would not be welcomed just yet.

Yes, his intention had been to take things very slowly until Gina called Emily's name.

'Emily!'

Hugh watched as she turned to the sound of

her name but this time it was Hugh's stomach that plummeted as he realised that it was Gina who would be driving Emily home.

Just yesterday Hugh had voiced his concerns about Gina to Alex and then Mr Eccleston, the head of anaesthetics. The decision as to whether or not to speak with Gina's boss had been eating at him for weeks. Hugh had been through medical school with Gina—they were good friends and he had always looked out for her.

But he had to look out for the patients first.

He could not turn his back so had voiced his concerns and the truth was tonight he wasn't sure that Gina hadn't been drinking, or even if she was on something else.

All he knew now was that he could not let Emily get into a car with Gina and, given the delicate nature of his complaint, neither could he share his concerns with Emily. He instead chose to act on the undeniable sexual tension between them.

'*I'm* taking you home.'

His words were very decisive and Emily

looked back at him. An alarm was ringing in her head, warning her to just walk away now, except there was something else signalling louder.

Instinct.

She had never been more aware of it. Simply, her instinct told her to accept the kiss that was nearing.

'Emily!' They could both hear Gina calling her name again, but this time it seemed to be coming from a very long way off.

She caught the fresh tang of him, a scent that had remained trapped in her senses since the first day they had met. Oh, where was her perfect man when she needed him? The one that didn't move her so.

Hugh lowered his head and his mouth brushed hers. Soft and warm, it made her own lips want to part like the Red Sea but she somehow held them closed. Except that meant she inhaled his scent, and the scent of Hugh was possibly more potent so she borrowed the wall behind her to lean on. His lips were more insistent now, nudging hers as his hands held her face, and finally their mouths commenced their first dance—a gentle dance at first to accustom themselves, then a playful dance that began to tease, but when their tongues met it was like an accelerant.

Hugh actually felt the shift. One minute they were kissing and the next their mouths belonged to each other. The party disappeared, the only noise was them—cool to his words she was hot to his mouth, Hugh felt as if he'd tripped and found a portal as he held the passion that burned in his arms. His hands left her face and moved to her hips without thought and were made very welcome for her bottom left the wall and the press of her body was as suggestive as his.

He pulled back but only because to continue would have them on the edge of indecent. Emily could taste his breath, see his lips wet from hers and she wanted to be back there now, yet she resisted the call of her body and moved her hips away from him.

Oh, it wasn't that Hugh was bad that terrified her, it was that he was so, so good.

'I really do have to go.'

She moved to the side and slipped past, and Hugh watched as she walked off, both trying to get his breath back and trying to ignore the fact he had been dismissed. Then he smothered the smile that came to his lips when Louise told Emily that Gina had just gone. 'She said you looked busy.'

There was a flush on Emily's cheeks but it wasn't from embarrassment, it was from arousal by the man who was now by her side.

'Let's go.'

It could have been an awkward ride home except Emily knew that she was possibly approaching the ride of her life.

Never, in all her twenty-three years had a man detonated her the way Hugh had.

His hand was on her thigh as they drove and she took no offence for hers was on his and it was suggestive down to her fingernails in a way she had never been before. The relief when he turned off the engine at the same time as he pulled up the handbrake had her snap off her seat belt in haste to return to his mouth.

'Emily…' His hand was up her skirt like two out-of-control teenagers and the spinning wheels in her head slowed as he halted. 'Not here.'

She was going to ask him in.

Sex.

Brilliant, sex and, and…

Emily pulled back her head and denied instinct.

'I'm going in…'

'Sure.' Hugh would, of course, rather she asked him in too but, well, this would be so worth the wait.

She watched his mouth move and offer dinner, a catch-up next week, though his hand between her thighs told her it would definitely end in bed and it was time to bring things to a halt.

'Hugh.' She let out a breath. 'I don't know…' She changed tack. 'It's just…' How could she deny the want that thrummed between them?

For Emily there was but one thing left to do so she came up with a rapid lie. 'I'm seeing someone.'

'Oh.'

'Gregory.'

'It's fine, I get it…' Though he didn't. Poor Gregory, Hugh thought as he reclaimed his hand, because five minutes from now he'd have had her knickers off.

'He's in Scotland, so we don't see each other as much as—'

'You really don't need to explain.'

And so the phantom Gregory was born.

When her father and Donna broke up in the New Year it was to Gregory she turned, rather than Hugh, though they did touch on it once, because Hugh came into the staffroom when Emily was on the phone.

'Donna, I get it that you have issues with my father but I don't understand what that has to do with me. If you don't want to see me that's fine but can I just take the twins to the park or for an ice cream every now and then…?' She turned in her chair and saw that Hugh had come in just as Donna told her that, no, she'd prefer Emily didn't have extra contact with the twins—she could see them when her father bothered to.

'Is she not letting you see the twins?' Hugh asked when she came off the phone.

'I can see them when they're with my dad, which isn't very often. I asked if I could take them out at the weekend but it unsettles them apparently.'

'Can she do that?'

'Of course she can.' Emily stood and went to walk past but Hugh caught her arm.

'Emily?'

'What?'

'Do you want…?' Hugh didn't really know what he was offering.

Emily did.

Yes, she did want.

She wanted to burst into tears, she wanted him to take her out and not cheer her up, just share…

She wanted to share with him.

Emily looked down at the fingers that still held her wrist.

Oh, he could hurt her, Emily thought, and then looked up to his eyes. He could really, really hurt her.

'I'll sort it out,' Emily said. 'Gregory is going to try and speak with her.'

At the mention of Gregory his hand disengaged from her arm.

For the next three months, every time Emily went to visit her mother Hugh was brought up to speed through vague conversations. However, just as he was starting to wonder about the fact that Gregory never seemed to come down to London, Emily actually found her perfect guy for real, so Gregory was swiftly dumped.

Marcus *was* perfect.

Dark haired, terribly serious, he was a social worker at the hospital and liked to hike at weekends. Sex happened on Saturdays, occasional

Tuesdays, and Emily developed solid calf muscles from trips up hillsides.

It was perfect for close to two years when the breaking news arrow shot across the hospital grapevine that Marcus had been found in a compromising position in the X-ray department with Heidi, the Swedish radiographer.

Hugh, now a senior registrar and going out with Olivia by then, expected tears in the staffroom, blushes and drama—the usual type of thing that happened with a very public break-up. With Emily that didn't happen, though...

Oh, she was a curious thing.

Emily just shrugged it off and got on with work.

The very next Monday they stood in Theatre and Emily glanced up as the alarm went off on the cardiac monitor when the anaesthetised patient kicked off a few ectopic heartbeats.

'All fine,' Rory, the anaesthetist, called as the patient's heart steadied back into a regular rhythm.

There were no flashing lights, no drama—it was hardly an event really.

And that was just how Emily liked things.

It was how she kept control.

CHAPTER ONE

'I DON'T WANT to work there.'

It was, for Emily, as simple as that.

She and Hugh had been working together for close to three years now and often caught up on a Monday. Now, in their lunch break, they sat in the staffroom at their favourite table, putting the world to rights.

'I think you'd be very good in Accident and Emergency,' Hugh said. 'Anyway, it's only for three months.'

'Well, why don't you go and work in Labour and Delivery for three months and then get back to me with that statement.'

'Fair point,' Hugh conceded.

'I'm going to speak to Miriam today and see if there's any way I can get out of doing it.'

Miriam, the head of Critical Nursing, had, last year, decided to rotate the staff on the units.

Emily had reluctantly done a three-month stint in ICU and had thought that would be the end of it, but Miriam had decided to press on with internally rotating the staff. Emily had been told that in June she would be commencing a term in Accident and Emergency.

Theatre was Emily's stomping ground. The thought of working in Emergency was unsettling—the drama of it, the emotion, the constant loaning out of your heart if you chose to empathise, or the burn-out that left you a tough bitch. Emily couldn't decide what was worse. She had no intention of revealing to Hugh the real reasons she was so opposed to the idea, so instead she changed the subject.

'So, is it true?' Hugh didn't reply to her question but Emily pushed on. 'Have you and Olivia broken up?'

'Yep.'

'I thought you two were happy.'

'We were,' Hugh said. 'When we were together.'

'What do you mean?'

It was Hugh who sat silent for a moment now. He and Olivia had been happy. Everyone had said how suited they were and, yes, their relationship had ticked most boxes.

Two boxes had been missing, though.

Olivia's jealousy and trust issues were one and as for the other…

He looked across the table to where Emily was peeling open her croissant and sprinkling more black pepper onto the cheese and tomato that filled it. She loved black pepper—there were always a couple of sachets in the pocket of her scrubs.

He knew a lot more about her than he had three years ago.

Just not enough.

'I don't know how to explain it, Em,' Hugh admitted. 'I don't know why Olivia felt that every time I was late home or out on a work do that there had to be more to it…'

'You do have a reputation,' Emily pointed out. As much as she liked catching up with Hugh, she loathed hearing about his life, his girlfriends, the wild parties and frequent holidays and weekends away.

Mondays were sometimes torture.

In fact, sometimes Emily dreaded them.

'Perhaps I do have a reputation around the hospital but I've never cheated when I'm seeing someone...' Hugh chose to go back a few years and watched a dull blush spread on her neck. 'If I am then I wouldn't so much as kiss another person.'

'Well...' Emily flustered a little. It was far too late, all these years on, to tell him there had never been a Gregory. It was far safer not to—that little black mark against her name was one she would happily wear if it kept her at a distance from Hugh. 'So what brought it to a head?'

'There's a conference coming up in a couple of months that Hadfield wants me to go on. I only mentioned it in passing but... The thing is, if I'm going to stand any chance of getting the consultancy then I really ought to go and concentrate—but Olivia seemed to think it was a good chance to have a couple of days' holiday, then she couldn't fathom why I might not want her to go with me...' His green eyes met Emily's. 'If I do get the consultancy position, things are only going to get busier for me. Call me selfish but I want to focus on my career and that means I can't be checking in every five minutes and reassuring someone that I'm behaving...' Hugh shook his head. 'Am I unreasonable?'

'No.' Emily fully agreed and she genuinely meant her words. She had long ago learnt from her parents that a million phone calls and texts meant little. 'If someone's going to cheat, they will.'

Hugh rolled his eyes. 'The point is, Em, I don't cheat. More to the point right now, Alex is pretty angry that I've broken up with Olivia and I want that promotion.' Hugh brooded for a moment. 'I got turned down last year.'

'Ouch,' Emily said.

'I get it that I perhaps wasn't ready then but I am ready now.'

'He can't judge whether or not you get the role on that.'

'I'm sure he wouldn't admit to it, but he's of the opinion that behind every great surgeon is a stable home life…' Hugh rolled his eyes and Emily laughed. 'I want that role,' Hugh said. Alex was a professor now and a consultancy position had officially opened up and Hugh could think of no one that he wanted to work alongside more. Alex was an amazing mentor. His technique and studies into laparoscopic surgery were right at the front of the game and every hour of every day Alex taught him something new.

'Behave for a few months, then!' Emily said. 'It really isn't that difficult.'

'Oh, but it is when you find yourself suddenly single.' Hugh drained his cup and then headed back to work. Emily sat alone for a while, pondering a suddenly single Hugh.

It was the time she loathed him most.

Or rather the time she loathed most.

Hugh worked hard and partied the same way.

If she didn't have to hear it on Monday in Theatre then it was all over bloody Facebook.

She had the next hour at the computer to work on the off-duty roster then she was down to scrub for Alex, but instead of heading to tackle the roster Emily looked over at Miriam, who was just heading out of the staffroom.

Instead of rinsing her cup and plate, Emily put them in the sink and caught up with her. 'Miriam, I wondered if I could have a word.'

'Now?' Miriam checked, and Emily nodded. This needed to be done.

They stepped into Miriam's office and Emily took a seat as Miriam gave her a thin smile. 'I can guess what this is about. I know that you're not keen to go to A and E.'

'Because I'm happy here,' Emily said.

'Emily, rotating the critical care staff has proved a success. Handovers are smoother, we're all more aware of the other departments' procedures...'

'I understand that,' Emily said, 'but I chose to be a theatre nurse.'

'And you're a very good one,' Miriam said. 'One who I hope will go far...' She left the rest unsaid but to Emily it was clear that if she wanted to go further in her career here, which she did, then she would have to comply. 'It's a couple of months away,' Miriam added. 'There's plenty of time to get used to the idea.'

Emily didn't want to get used to the idea, she liked being used to *here*!

'Any luck with Miriam?' Hugh asked at the end of the day as Emily came out of the changing room dressed for the outside world. Hugh was looking pretty drained—he'd been operating since eight a.m. and now would be heading up to the wards to check on his post-operative patients.

'Nope.' Emily's jaw tensed and she let out a tense breath. 'If I want to get on—'

'Ha,' Hugh interrupted. 'Don't complain about that to me—at least you don't have Alex as your boss. I need a wife if I want to get on.'

'When we're in charge we'll change the world,' Emily said as they walked together.

Hugh was heading up to ICU, Emily for home, and it felt like a long time till next Monday for Hugh.

Hugh was possibly the one person who *did* like Mondays. Sure, he and Emily caught up during the week at various times but Monday was Alex's rostered operating day and on the days that Emily wasn't there he missed her.

Yes, Hugh wanted to finally move things on between them and give this *almost* romance its wings. He wanted a nice table between them and a waiter whose arm would probably drop off as he cracked enough pepper to satisfy Emily.

Okay, Hugh decided as they walked down the long corridor, whatever happened, he would not let it affect their friendship.

'You do realise,' Hugh said as they reached the swing doors that would take them out of Theatre and to their separate destinations, 'that this is the first time in three years that we've both been single at the same time.'

Nice opening! Hugh was just silently congratulating himself when Emily delivered her response.

'Well, I don't know about you but I'm staying that way,' Emily said, shutting down the conversation as firmly as the black doors swung closed behind them. ''Night, Hugh, it was nice working with you today.'

Was he missing something?

Hugh just watched as she walked off.

Did he have body odour that only Emily could smell?

They liked each other!

They fancied each other!

He could taste it.

If only she'd let him.

'Problem?' Alex asked, as he came out and saw his junior standing with a puzzled frown on his face.

'More a mystery,' Hugh said. 'One I intend to work out.'

He couldn't, though.

It would seem Emily was serious about staying single and for two whole months she did just that.

Till Hugh decided they might need a little helping hand.

CHAPTER TWO

'ARE YOU COMING to Emily's leaving do on Friday?' Louise asked Hugh, and Emily rather hoped the answer would be no—a meal at Imelda's and a few drinks afterwards would probably be a bit tame for Hugh.

'Can we do the swab count before I start to close?' Hugh said, instead of answering.

Nothing distracted him, Emily noted.

It was the mark of a brilliant surgeon.

Hugh chatted and joked but when it mattered he concentrated totally. As boring as the swab count and equipment check might be, it was necessary to ensure that nothing was left inside the patient before the surgeon closed, and Hugh took it seriously.

The counts all tallied.

'It isn't Emily's leaving do,' Hugh said, as he started to close the incision. 'She's only going to be working in A and E for three months but, yes, I'll be there. Actually, Alex and his wife are coming too, if they can get a babysitter.'

'It's just a few drinks…' Emily frowned because why the hell was Alex coming, let alone his wife? 'As you said, it's not even a leaving do.'

Except, unbeknown to anyone but Emily, it very possibly was her leaving do.

Emily hadn't yet handed in her notice but next Wednesday she was going to Cornwall for a week and had decided if, after a break, she still felt the same way about working in A and E, then that was what she would do.

'You're going to be missed,' Hugh said. Emily saw his lovely green eyes over the mask and, yes, he was speaking the truth both personally and professionally. Emily was efficient, incredibly efficient, some might say pedantic and others set in her ways, but Theatre worked well with pedantic nurses. 'Mondays won't be the same.'

'Actually, they shall, for a little while at least,'

Emily said. 'I'm back working here on Monday as an extra shift—they haven't found my replacement yet. The nurse who was coming here from A and E resigned.'

'When do you go on holiday?' Louise asked.

'Next Wednesday,' Emily answered. 'A whole week of doing nothing but walking and reading. I can't wait.'

'There's some nice weather predicted...' Louise smiled.

'Which means it will rain!' Hugh's comment was dry.

'I don't care,' Emily said. 'I just want to read and walk on the beach and relax.'

'Well, you'll need it before you go to A and E,' Louise said.

'How are we doing, Rory?' Hugh glanced over at the anaesthetist as a couple of alarms started to sound.

'All good. How much longer?'

'Done,' Hugh said.

Yes, it was a very small world in Theatre. Emily headed to the large staffroom. She was the first there but everyone would soon come in. Rarely did anyone go to the canteen—it was too much trouble to change shoes and things. She turned and gave a brief smile as Hugh came in and she got out her lunch from the fridge but, as they sat down, instead of their usual catch-up Hugh got paged to go up to a ward.

'Damn,' Hugh said. 'I wanted to talk to you.'

'I'm sure it will keep.'

Hugh thought for a moment as he answered his page. Emily was right, it would keep and what he had to ask her would probably go better with wine!

'Can I borrow you for ten minutes on Friday night?'

'Borrow me?'

'Well, I know you'll be busy but there's something that I want to ask you away from everyone else.'

'Like what?'

'Not here.'

'Have you got another rash?' Emily smirked.

'Ha-ha.'

They both smiled as they remembered the day when Hugh, for once, had struggled to focus. Emily had been scrub nurse and had frowned as a usually together Hugh had breathed loudly beside her, sweat beading on his forehead as he kept moving from one foot to the other. The second the operation had been over he had fled and, walking past the male changing rooms on the way to the staffroom, Emily had seen his frantic face peer out.

'Emily...' he'd hissed. 'I need some antihistamine.'

'What?'

'Now. IM...'

'An injection?'

Hugh let the towel slip a fraction and Emily's eyes widened at the sight of the angry red welts and urticarial rash spreading down his buttocks.

'Believe me, Emily, that's not the worst of it...'

'I don't want to see the rest.'

Oh, my!

Emily had returned with the injection and

some hydrocortisone cream for Hugh to put on *himself* and had happily stabbed him.

'Maybe it was the shaving cream…'

She didn't want to know that he'd shaved, or that *she*, whoever *she* was this week, had shaved him. Emily was tired of the glimpses into his love life.

'Have you changed your washing powder?' Emily asked instead.

'No.' Hugh shook his head and thought for a moment. 'Though I did buy the liquid one.'

As it turned out, he had bought the triple-strength liquid one!

Happily, his reaction had calmed and the theatre list had gone ahead, Emily trying and failing not to dwell on the fact that he was naked and bald beneath his scrubs.

'What will I do without you?' Hugh asked, still smiling as he recalled that day.

'Inject your own antihistamine!'

'That was a long time ago, Emily.'

Yet she remembered it like it was yesterday.

The hurt, the jealousy, the itch of her own that she simply refused to scratch.

'If I don't catch up with you properly,' Hugh said, 'then I'll see you Friday.'

'Okay.'

Friday found her in the staff changing room, getting ready to go to Imelda's, a nice casual bar that did amazing food and, on weekends, had a band.

Emily was tired before the night had even started but, given it was her leaving do, she did her best not to show it.

Louise and she changed at work. Emily into a tube skirt and top, Louise into the tightest red dress and high heels. They were close friends now.

Louise looked stunning, especially when she topped it off with dark red lipstick.

'Tart,' Emily said.

'A happy tart, though.' Louise smiled.

'Are you?' Emily checked. Louise was coming out of a terrible break up and had been very subdued but finally she seemed to be finding herself again.

'I'm getting there,' Louise said. 'Come on.'

They walked out of Theatre and down the corridor and there, coming towards them, was Anton, the new Italian obstetrician who had hearts thumping everywhere.

'Hi, Anton.' Louise smiled.

'Evening.'

'We're heading over to Imelda's—there will be quite a few of us.' Louise gave a smile that could be described as sweet were it not for the wanton red lips, but it was barely returned.

'I'm working,' Anton said, and strode off.

'You're subtle,' Emily commented.

'He's fresh off the plane,' Louise said. 'I was just doing my social duty. God, don't you want to just grab him by the stethoscope and climb up it?'

'No.' Emily laughed. 'Not in the least, he's far too moody for me.'

They had booked a room at the back of the restaurant and it was actually really nice to be among friends and colleagues. Hugh hadn't arrived but that was possibly a good thing as Emily didn't really want to meet whomever it was that he was dating now.

Surely he was seeing someone.

Two months single for Hugh would be a record.

Or maybe he was just enjoying the off-season and sleeping around, though, for once, Emily had heard nothing on the grapevine about him.

Emily sat between Louise and Alex's wife Jennifer and, as it turned out, Louise had news of her own.

'It will be my leaving do next,' Louise said.

'You've just done your internal rotation.' Emily frowned.

'No, mine will be for real.' Louise's blue eyes were shining. 'I'm going to work in Maternity.'

'When did you decide that?'

'It's been brewing for a while,' Louise admitted. 'I can't wait to get back there.'

'It wouldn't have anything to do with Anton?' Emily teased.

'God, no! I'm not that shallow,' Louise said, because despite walking a little on the wild side she took her work seriously. 'I'm just ready for a change. I love the Caesareans we have in Theatre and lately it's just not been enough for me. I want to be more involved with the mothers and babies.' She smiled at Emily. 'You like the cool of Theatre, don't you?'

'I do,' Emily said.

'I just want back out there…' Louise admitted.

'Have you told Miriam?'

'Not yet.' Louise winced at the very thought. 'I haven't actually applied for a position yet, I'm just putting out feelers, but I don't think Miriam will be very pleased—a lot of staff have left recently.'

'Well, she should have thought of that before she moved the goalposts for getting a promotion,' Emily said, but as Louise went to open her mouth to respond she stopped her. 'If another person tells me I'll be great and that it will fly by, I won't be responsible for my response.'

'I'll say nothing, then.' Louise smiled. 'I'll get you a drink instead.'

Hugh arrived just as dessert was being served. Emily was sitting chatting to Alex and Jennifer when Hugh came over. He gave her a kiss on the cheek, which was a bit uncalled for, but, yes, at the time Emily put it down to the fact that it was her leaving do.

'Sorry, I tried to get here earlier...' Hugh said.

'It's fine.'

'I got stuck up on ICU...'

'Really, Hugh, it's fine,' Emily said. She had no idea why he was making such a fuss about not getting here on time—a lot of her colleagues were only dropping in for a drink after all.

'I'll get you a drink,' Hugh offered.

'I don't want one...' Emily said, only Hugh wasn't listening. He headed off to the bar and returned with something very icy and bubbly and so not what Emily wanted. She'd had a bit too much icy and bubbly and she wasn't a big drinker at the best of times but everyone seemed determined to buy her one tonight.

'You'll be dancing on the tables in a few weeks,' Hugh said, squeezing a chair into the tiny gap between herself and Louise.

'Why?'

'I'm here tomorrow night with the emergency mob for Gina's thirtieth—believe me, the theatre staff's nights outs are very civilised in comparison to that lot.'

Emily went over to speak with Connor, another theatre nurse, but Hugh was like an annoying wasp and hanging around her like some lovesick teenager. Frankly, he was starting to really annoy her.

'What?' Emily snapped, when still Hugh hovered. 'What's going on, Hugh?'

'Can I have that ten minutes now?'

'Fine,' Emily sighed, and turned to him.

'Outside.'

'Hugh, it's my leaving do, I'm not going to—'

'Ten minutes.'

Emily headed outside.

'I want to ask you something. You know what

I said about us still being single—do you want to give us a try?'

Emily was taken aback by his directness.

'No.'

'Can I ask why?'

'I don't need to give a reason.' She went to head back but Hugh caught her arm.

'I've still got nine minutes of your time left.'

'Use them wisely, then,' Emily said.

'Okay.' Hugh took a breath. 'Second question. Would you consider pretending to go out with me?'

'Pretend?'

'I want the consultancy. Alex likes you…'

'That's the most ridiculous idea I've ever heard. He'd soon find out you were lying.'

'Not if we're clever about it.'

'No.'

'Give me one good reason why not,' Hugh said.

She looked at Hugh, his hair flopping over his eyes, his green eyes smiling, and he was just so cocky and assured, so utterly at ease with himself that Emily could tell he was a touch taken back that she hadn't jumped at the chance to be his fake girlfriend.

'You know what Alex is like,' Hugh persisted. 'He hasn't come right out and said it but the writing's on the wall—he wants to know that my party days are over before he'll give me the consultancy.'

'But they're not over,' Emily pointed out.

'They could be for the next couple of months.'

'I'm not handing over two months of my life to be your fake girlfriend—'

'No,' Hugh interrupted. 'I'm not asking for two months, I'm asking for a couple of Saturday nights and the occasional wedding. I could come down to Cornwall at the weekend and kick things off with a few photos. You're not seeing anyone and surely...' He hesitated.

'Go on.'

'It will be exciting.'

'Really!' Emily was having trouble keeping an incredulous smile from her lips. 'Tell me how.'

'Well...' Hugh actually had the decency to

look a touch uncomfortable. 'You said that your holiday was going to be a bit boring...'

'No, I didn't,' Emily corrected him. 'I said my holiday was going to be very quiet, which, somewhere between here...' she tapped her lips '...and there...' she tapped his forehead '...you translated as boring. A week in a cottage, doing nothing, isn't boring, Hugh.'

'It certainly wouldn't be if I came along.' Hugh grinned.

'Would I have to sleep with you?' Emily asked. 'In this little charade of yours, would sex be on the books?'

'If you want to,' Hugh said, mildly surprised that Emily had so readily brought it up. 'If you're saddled with being my girlfriend, there would have to be perks...'

'Your ego knows no bounds.'

'Think about it,' Hugh said.

'I have,' Emily said, and started to walk back inside, 'and the answer's no.'

'Come on, Emily...'

'Was that the reason for the kisses and the

"Sorry I couldn't get here earlier" and following me about?'

'Yep.'

'I tell you one thing,' Emily said, 'if we were going out then we wouldn't be for long if you followed me about like that.'

'I know.' Hugh laughed. 'I was just trying to get Alex used to the possibility that we were on with each other…I was actually starting to annoy myself.'

Had he left it at that, all would have been okay.

If a glass of champagne hadn't been thrust into her hand by Louise then possibly things wouldn't have unravelled but, unknown to anyone, she was battling tears.

His fake girlfriend.

Bloody cheek, Emily thought.

She wanted to be his real one.

So why hadn't she simply said yes when he'd asked to give them a try? Or had that been just a ruse for Alex's benefit too?

Damn you, Hugh!

Emily knew she was being contrary, she knew that over the years Hugh must at times have felt like some baffled semaphore signaller as she'd flirted and waved red flags while her mouth had done its best to refute what her body said.

After the break-up with Marcus it had been relatively easy to move on, but getting over Hugh… Emily tried to imagine working alongside him when she had been relegated to being his ex and—fake girlfriend or real one—she knew that one day the inevitable would happen.

But if she wasn't working there…

Stop it, Emily told herself, determined not to go there. It was a relief when people started to leave and Emily could go and retrieve her bag. Hugh's strange offer had left her all unsettled and quite simply she wanted home.

Only Hugh had other ideas.

As she stepped out onto the street she heard him call her name.

'Emily…' Hugh caught her arm. 'Have you thought about it?'

'Sorry?'

'You know…' Hugh said, moving her into the shadows, 'what we were talking about before.'

'I've already given you my answer.'

'Oh, come on, Emily, it would be fun.'

'How?'

Emily stood there. A taxi was approaching and her friends were calling for her to join them and there was Alex and his wife Jennifer leaving.

She knew that because Hugh chose his moment and started kissing her neck.

'Foreshadowing,' Hugh said, in between kisses.

'Or just adding to your reputation,' Emily said, trying to ignore the sensations his lips were delivering, trying not to be moved by the feel of Hugh's hands on her waist.

Little butterfly kisses were being delivered to her cheeks and her lips were starting to thrum hungrily in anticipation as, three years on, the master picked up the lead and offered a decadent walk. And just as she had when last they'd kissed, Emily had to come up with a rapid reason why it wouldn't work.

Before lips met she had to come up with a reason or she'd be dragging him by the hair to the taxi and up the stairs to her bed.

Or would she let him drag her.

Oh, my!

She was again starting to consider the possibilities, just tossing all warnings aside and going along with his ridiculous plan. It was the feeling of suddenly wavering that had Emily pull back.

'I can't do it.'

'I'm waiting for the reason.'

'I can't do it because...' Come on, think, Emily, she told herself, come up with one very good reason why it would be an impossible idea. And then her champagne- and Hugh-befuddled brain found a solution. 'Because I don't like you,' Emily said. Hugh just grinned.

'No, I mean it, I don't really enjoy your company so...' Shut up, Emily, her mind said, but she simply couldn't stop. Emily could actually

see the frown between his eyes as the words hit.
'I put up with you at work, of course, it's part
of my job, but...'

'Okay.' He stepped back.

'You asked why not,' Emily said. 'You asked
for one good reason...'

'I get the message,' Hugh said. 'Finally.'

Emily closed her eyes, very aware that she
had handled that terribly, then she forced them
open and took a breath, knowing that she had
to apologise.

But how?

How could she explain that she didn't like his
company at times because it ate her up inside?
How could she explain when he was inches
from her mouth that her feelings for him terrified her?

'Hugh...'

'Let's just leave it.'

They walked over to the line of taxis and
Hugh opened the door of one for her.

'Hugh...' Emily said as she got in.

''Night, Emily.' He closed the door.

All the way home Emily kicked herself. She couldn't have handled that more badly if she had tried but the near kiss had actually caused her to panic.

Get over yourself.

Maybe it was time to, Emily thought. Perhaps she could apologise properly on Monday.

Maybe even explain how she felt?

That she was actually terrified to get close to anyone.

She paid the taxi driver and headed to her home, and for the first time her resolution wavered, the cloak of self-preservation almost slid off, for she wanted the feelings Hugh triggered and yet she knew, from his undeniable track record, that soon they'd be done.

Time to take a risk, Emily.

In fact, it was long overdue that she did.

She was just pulling him up on her computer, just trying to convince herself to wait till tomorrow to attempt contact because she'd made enough of a mess of things tonight already.

Then she saw that she had a message.

From her dad.

Emily, I tried to call.
I've got some good news, two bits of good news actually.

Emily read the message, her eyes filling with tears as she heard that her dad was marrying again and soon, because—guess what—Cathy was pregnant!

A little brother or sister for you, her dad tossed in, and she was very glad she'd missed his call because she felt like screaming.

Would it be like it had been with the twins all over again?

She actually ached to see them but it wasn't just the blood relations that hurt. There had been so many girlfriends and along with them their children, and it was much the same with her mum.

'I don't want to go to your wedding.' Emily said it out loud as she stared at the screen, though she knew she'd do the right thing and be there, more in the hope of seeing the twins, though.

If Donna let them attend.

That was why she was like this, Emily reminded herself. That was why she let no one in.

She checked her reminders. It was her half-sister Abby's birthday tomorrow and though she had sent a gift in the post Emily posted a message on her mum's timeline.

She flicked through some images; saw Abby smiling with her own dad's children from a previous relationship.

There wasn't enough wood in a forest to map Emily's family tree.

It was always *the one*, her parents told her when they met the latest love of their life.

This time they were sure.

Until it was over.

Emily allowed herself one look at the smiling image of Hugh on her screen and then clicked off.

Hugh was a sure-fire recipe for disaster.

She was right to refuse herself a taste.

CHAPTER THREE

FOR ONCE HUGH wasn't looking forward to Monday.

And it wasn't just Emily's revelation that had soured the weekend!

The accident and emergency do *had* been a little wild and Hugh had again had to put out an increasingly regular fire named Gina.

He'd gone round yesterday to speak to her and she'd done her best to convince him it had just been a one-off, that she hadn't been the only one who'd had too much to drink.

True.

And, yes, it had been her thirtieth birthday after all.

Yet Hugh wasn't so sure it was just the drinking that was the problem.

Three years ago when he'd voiced his concerns first to Alex and then to Mr Eccleston, the head of Anaesthetics, he had been taken seriously. Gina had actually cried on him about the unknown person who had threatened her career.

It had all come to nothing and it had eaten Hugh up since then that possibly he had jumped the gun because Gina really was an amazing doctor and she had proved it over and over.

Just lately, though, Hugh felt that things were sliding again.

Driving to work, he took a call from his sister. 'Is everything okay?' Hugh instantly checked.

'Of course. Why wouldn't it be?' Kate answered.

'It's not even seven a.m.'

'Well, I knew you'd be on your way to work and I don't like to trouble you there.'

'You can call me any time, Kate.'

'Hugh, can you take your social-worker voice off? Just because I've had a baby it doesn't mean that there has to be a problem.'

Easy for you to say, Hugh thought, pulling up at traffic lights. Three years ago Hugh had taken Emily's advice and practically frogmarched Kate to her doctor, and still, all these years on, what had happened in Kate's dark teenage years ate at him.

'So, what are you calling for?' Hugh asked instead.

'We've booked Billy's christening,' Kate said, 'for the end of June.' Hugh grimaced when she gave him the date. He was quite sure he was on take that weekend and he'd already swapped his roster once to accommodate an upcoming wedding that he wouldn't miss for the world.

He'd actually given Kate a list of his available dates when she had started to talk about making plans for the christening.

Let it go, Hugh, he told himself as the lights changed.

Yet he always let it go around Kate.

'The thing is, I'm actually—' Hugh attempted, but Kate cut in.

'We want you to be godfather.'

'Oh!' Hugh didn't know what to say at first and then he said the right thing. 'I'd be delighted to.'

So there was no getting out of it, then.

Damn.

Hugh loved his sister and nephews very, very much; it was just the timing of things that was a serious issue. How the hell could he ask for another Sunday off?

'Will you be bringing someone?' Kate asked.

'Probably not.'

'I'll need to know for the restaurant.'

'No, then.'

'Hugh?' Kate checked, because there was a terse edge to his voice.

'It's just a bit of a sore point at the moment.'

'I thought you and Olivia were well over and done with.'

'We are,' Hugh said, 'well, I am.'

'Is she still calling?'

'Now and then.'

'So what's the sore point?'

'I've got to go, Kate,' Hugh said. 'I'll give you a call in the week. Thanks for asking me to be godfather, it means a lot.'

It did.

Hugh pulled into the work car park and saw the rare sight of Emily's car. Usually she took public transport but occasionally she brought the bomb in.

There was the sore point.

He didn't buy it that Emily didn't like him.

He knew that she did.

And he liked her.

He had from the first day they had met. Hugh liked strong women, strong, independent women, and Emily was all of that.

Oh, not the shaved-head, unshaved-leg kind, it was her independence along with her femininity that continued to draw him in. With Emily he was himself, without qualification, without having to apologise if something he had said or done might have caused offence.

'Hugh!' He turned at the sound of Alex's voice and waited while he caught up with him.

'Hi, Alex, good weekend?'

'A very good weekend,' Alex said, as the men walked through the car park. 'Jennifer's mother came for a visit and has agreed to stay with us for the summer.'

'That's good news, is it?' Hugh smiled because wasn't your mother-in-law coming for an extended visit most husbands' idea of hell?

'It is.' Alex nodded. 'With all my work and studying I've let things slide a bit, I feel, but we've had a talk and with Jennifer's mum here for a few months we can make a bit more of my days off. Jennifer needs a break.'

Hugh glanced over. He had nothing but admiration for the man—from toddlers to teenagers, Alex dealt with it all, as well as study and research and holding down such a demanding position. Hugh wanted that consultancy position. There wasn't a day that went by that he didn't learn something from Alex, and not just in the operating theatre.

'You have to work at anything if you want it to be successful, Hugh,' Alex said, 'and I'm not just talking about the salaried stuff.'

Hugh wasn't sure if that was a small dig about his and Olivia's break-up but, then again, he was surprised that Alex was talking about bumpy times at home to him. 'Well, I hope you both have a great summer.'

'We shall,' Alex said. 'Right now I'm off to breakfast with Clem. I'll see you in theatre.'

Emily hadn't been looking forward to Monday either.

She walked into the staffroom and there was Hugh sitting in his usual spot. After making a coffee, Emily went and joined him, just as she usually did. 'About what I said the other night—' Emily started.

'Your shift doesn't start for another ten minutes,' Hugh interrupted, 'so you don't have to talk to me yet.'

'Hugh, it came out all wrong.'

'I think you made yourself very clear.'

'I do like you,' Emily said, her cheeks going red, 'just not in that way.'

'Okay.'

'And if we did suddenly start going out...' She just gave a shake of her head and tried to explain how it could never work. 'I've got my dad's wedding next month. Do you really want to go to that circus? Because he'd know about us too.'

'How?'

'Because he follows me on Facebook,' Emily said. 'It's pretty much how we communicate and Mum follows me too. It would just all get too complicated.'

'Fine.' He looked at her and she could see the hurt in his eyes. 'I shan't keep you. I'll see you in Theatre.'

'Hugh,' Emily called him before he could walk off. 'I'm not in Theatre today, I'm rostered for Anaesthetics.'

'You don't have to run your schedule by me.'

'I'm just explaining that I'm not avoiding you, I'm filling in this morning so I didn't get to do the placements...'

Hugh didn't answer, he just walked off.

What a mess, Emily thought as she made her way to the anaesthetic room. It was a small annexe that led to two of the theatres. Here the patient would be anaesthetised and intubated before being taken into the operating theatre. She was in for a busy morning. First was Ernest Bailey and though his was a long case, before Hugh's next one there were two epidurals scheduled for two planned Caesareans.

Emily smiled when she saw that it was Rory who was on. He was pulling up medication so that everything would be ready, well out of sight of the patient, and they chatted for a moment as they set up. 'I thought I was down to work with Gina,' Emily said.

'And I thought I had Monday off,' Rory responded, and then explained that he'd been called in the early hours to come in. 'She called in sick—I think she had a bit too much Hugh on Saturday night.'

Emily simply rolled her eyes—maybe Hugh had been busy trying to persuade Gina to pull the wool over Alex's eyes for a few weeks.

Maybe the two of them had got it on.

Emily bit her lip as she looked at the theatre list. That burn of jealousy was low in her chest and reminded her how much getting too close to Hugh could only inevitably hurt.

He *was* a friend, though, despite what she had said the other night, and that was something she didn't want to lose.

Rory was explaining to Emily that Ernest would be going to ICU after his surgery when Hugh came in.

'He's not here yet,' Emily said, because usually the patient would be here by now and waiting for a brief word with the surgeon before going under.

'I know,' Hugh said. 'He's taking his time to say goodbye to his wife. Poor old boy doesn't really want the surgery but his wife has told him she wants him there for their golden wedding anniversary...' He paused as Ernest was wheeled in. 'Good morning, Mr Bailey.' Hugh was lovely to the man. 'How's Hannah?'

'Fussing,' Ernest said.

'And how are you feeling?'

'Thirsty!' came another one-word answer as Hugh checked again the markings he had made on Ernest's stomach. 'When can I get a cup of tea?'

'That's a bit of a way off for you,' Hugh said. 'I'll come and see you in Recovery after the operation and then later again on ICU.'

Ernest rolled his eyes. All he wanted to know was when his next drink would be, but soon he was under and Emily moved him through to the theatre and then came back to prepare the room for the next patient.

'Morning,' Emily said, as Anton and Declan, another anaesthetist, came in just as Emily had finished setting up for the epidural.

'Change of plan.' Declan smiled, unlike Anton, who just got straight down to business.

'We're going attempt a vaginal delivery in Theatre,' Anton said. 'Then we will do the planned cases.'

He went into Theatre to get ready and Emily rolled her eyes at Declan. 'Nice of the labour ward to let us know,' she said, just as the phone rang with that very news.

It was just a busy morning, punctuated by

the sound of a woman grunting and screaming. Louise was in her element, Emily was wincing and Rory laughed when Hugh came in once Ernest's surgery was over.

'Lovely background noise,' Hugh said. 'I'm just going to speak to Ernest's wife and then I'll have a quick drink. I've sent down for the next one.'

'Mr Bailey didn't take long,' Emily commented.

'It went better than expected,' Hugh said. 'I didn't end up doing a colostomy, he'll be pleased about that.'

As an ear-splitting scream filled the morning. Rory came in and laughed when he saw Emily's reaction. 'Is that with an epidural?' Emily asked him.

'Apparently she doesn't want any drugs.' Rory peered through the window into Theatre. 'Declan's just gone in, so maybe she's changed her mind. No, it looks like Anton's going to use forceps.'

'Oh, my,' Emily said.

'Is childbirth not for you, lovely Emily?' Rory asked, because Emily was the opposite of Louise and avoided that side of Theatre whenever possible.

'Not even with drugs,' Emily said. 'God, listen to Anton!'

It sounded like a football match was taking place, with the woman screaming, Anton urging her on and even Louise was cheering. Then there was a long stretch of silence, followed by lusty screams.

'Phew,' Emily said. 'I can uncross my legs now!' But Hugh didn't laugh at her joke, as he usually would have, and Emily remembered that they weren't talking.

'The next one up is very nervous,' Hugh said to Rory. 'I'll come and have a word with her before she goes under.'

'I ordered her a strong pre-op,' Rory commented, 'though I think it's the mother who needs it.'

Emily chose not to grab a coffee and spend another uncomfortable ten minutes with Hugh.

Instead she opted for a cola from the vending machine before setting up for the next patient—Jessica O'Farrell, an eighteen-year-old in for an exploratory laparoscopy.

'Mum wants to come in while she goes under.' Connor put his head through the doors and gave Rory a wry smile. 'I've said no but she's asked me to double-check!'

Rory shook his head. 'I've already spoken to Jessica about this. Mum's more stressed than her.'

Hugh was soon back from his quick coffee break and asked where the patient was as he was ahead of schedule and hoping to fit another patient onto the end of the list.

'Connor is just bringing her in now,' Emily answered, but as the trolley was wheeled in, for a second Emily froze.

She had been Jessica Albert when Emily had known her but of course her name might have changed all these years on.

'Emily!' Jessica's tears halted and the surprise in her voice had Hugh look at Emily for her reaction, but she just stood there as Jessica's tears actually stopped in mid-stream. 'It *is* you.'

'Jessica!' Hugh watched as Emily pushed out a smile but though it was a wide one, Hugh could see the shock in Emily's eyes and that her smile was guarded.

In all Emily's years of nursing it had never happened. Well, once an uncle had had a hip replacement, but she'd been expecting to see him.

This, though, was completely unexpected and Jessica wasn't even a relation.

She had once felt like one, though.

Today, had she been scrubbing in, as was her usual, Emily might not have even know that the patient was the Jessica she had known all those years ago. Thirteen years was a long time and with the different name and with her eyes closed, as they would have been in Theatre, Emily might not have even recognised her.

Emily pushed back the wave of emotion that threatened to knock her off course and walked over to the young woman. 'How are you?' Emily said, and then gave a little laugh. 'Well, that's a silly question, given that you're about to have surgery.'

'I've been dreading it,' Jessica said. 'I'm so scared of having an anaesthetic.'

'A lot of people are.' Emily squeezed her hand. 'Rory's on today and he's amazing, he'll take such good care of you. Have you met him?'

'He came and saw me this morning.' Jessica looked over at Rory and then back at Emily. 'Will you be there?'

'I'll be with you while you're put to sleep,' Emily said, and then bit her bottom lip as Jessica looked at Hugh.

'Emily and I were sisters...'

Hugh smiled back, though of course he didn't really understand. He was pleased to see his patient looking a lot more relaxed but right now he was more concerned about the nurse because Emily's face was chalk white and he watched as Jessica turned back to Emily. 'I've looked you up a few times,' Jessica admitted. 'I was going to friend you on Facebook but I didn't know if I'd be welcome...'

'I've tried to look you up too,' Emily said, 'though no wonder I didn't get very far, as that your surname's changed.'

'Mum married again and I took Mike's surname.'

Emily hesitated. She didn't really want to know how Katrina was doing and yet there was a small part of her that did. 'How is your mum?'

'She's good,' Emily said. 'She's happy. Well, I think she is.'

Does she ever mention me? Emily wanted to ask. And does she ever give me so much as a passing thought?

Tears were starting to sting at the back of Emily's eyes and she quickly turned away and busied herself with the medicines she had already pulled up—she certainly didn't want to add to Jessica's difficult morning with her own gush of emotion.

Thankfully Hugh seemed to realise that Emily was struggling and he started chatting away to Jessica, telling her that it wouldn't be a long procedure and he'd see her again when she woke up.

Hugh went to go. Rory had administered a stronger sedative, but the emotion in Jessica's voice in the moment before she went under had Hugh pause at the door. 'I missed you so much.'

Emily stared into her eyes and was honest in her response. 'I missed you too.'

Oh, how she had.

They had been weekend and holiday sisters and losing Jessica and even Katrina had been a hurt that had gone unacknowledged by all. And there had been many more losses since then.

Emily held Jessica's hand as she slid under and then helped wheel her through to the theatre and onto the operating table.

She glanced over to Hugh, who was scrubbing up, and he gave a small nod that said he'd take good care.

He always did.

Hugh worked on smaller procedures himself yet more and more he was honing his skills and was ready for that next step.

As he performed the procedure, an investigative laparoscopy for recurrent abdominal pain, Emily was the furthest thing from his mind.

He carefully checked the abdominal cavity and organs. Jessica had undergone many investigations and all had come back as normal.

As was this.

With the procedure over and Jessica being moved to Recovery, Hugh headed over there to check on Ernest.

'He looks terrible...' Hannah, his wife, was by the trolley, being comforted by their daughter, Laura.

'He's just had surgery, Mum, he was never going to be looking his best.' Laura tried to reassure her mother but her eyes were anxious when they met Hugh's. 'I know you warned us about the tubes and things but Mum didn't realise just how many there would be.'

'I should never had made him go through with it,' Hannah fretted. 'He didn't want the operation...'

'He's actually doing very well,' Hugh said, checking through the observations. 'I know it was a big decision but you both made it,' Hugh said gently. 'From what I've seen of your husband, he wouldn't be talked into anything he didn't want to do.'

He spent a few minutes reassuring Hannah but, glancing at Jessica, whose mother was being let in, his mind returned to Emily.

It was none of his business, Hugh told himself. Emily had made it very clear that she wanted no more than the relationship they had at work. Even so, he couldn't help listening to the conversation that was taking place.

'Emily's here…' They were the first words Jessica said as she struggled to sit up and take off her oxygen as a nurse gently kept her lying down.

'Emily?' Katrina said. Hugh wasn't just idly listening, he was watching and not even attempting to hide that he was.

'Emily,' Jessica said again. 'She's a nurse here. Maybe you could see her, say hello…'

Katrina shook her head. 'There's no need for that. How are you?'

'But Emily's here!' Groggy from anaesthetic, Jessica had no reserves and started pulling her oxygen mask off. 'Why wouldn't you want to see her?'

'Go back to sleep.' Katrina smiled, replacing the mask. 'You're a bit confused from all the medicine.'

Nice get-out, Mum, Hugh thought, but then he got back to business and headed over to let Jessica's mother know how the procedure had gone.

Yes, he should be cross with Emily, Hugh thought a little while later, or at the very least sulk and take his lunch elsewhere, but he could see her sitting, pretending to read a magazine, and Hugh knew she'd been crying.

'How was your morning?' Hugh asked, taking his usual seat.

'Busy,' Emily said. 'You've got a big afternoon coming up,' she added, because he and

Alex were doing an aneurism repair, but Hugh shook his head.

'Not any more. Rory wasn't happy with his blood work, but maybe tonight...' Hugh yawned and then looked at her swollen eyes. 'You know, if I was a friend, instead of someone you tolerated because you're paid to, you could talk to me about this morning.'

Emily didn't want to talk about that morning but she was glad of the chance to address Friday night. 'Hugh, I really am sorry about that. It came out all wrong. I just don't want to mess up our friendship...'

'You nearly did!' Hugh said, his voice serious, and Emily nodded. 'So what was this morning about? I know that it's hard when a relative comes in.'

'She's not a relative, though,' Emily said, with more than a dash of bitterness, and then decided it couldn't hurt to explain. 'When my parents' marriage broke up my dad moved down here and moved in with Katrina, Jessica's mum. I used to come down once a month, half the holidays…'

'How old were you?'

'Twelve,' Emily said. 'I didn't like Katrina at first but I was always nice to her and my dad made sure to let me know she'd be my stepmum once the divorce was through and that this was my new family. I loved Jessica from the start, though. When I was there we shared a room. She was only little but we used to have such a laugh and then one weekend I came down to stay and found out that Katrina and my dad had split up.'

'Did you not see them after that?'

'Nope.' Emily shook her head. 'I asked where they were, but it didn't matter apparently, and clearly I didn't matter enough to Katrina to stay in touch…' Emily closed her eyes as she recalled how easily people that she had been told to love, to treat as family, to care for had been removed from her life. 'It was just the start of it. After Katrina, Dad met someone else and then someone else, then it was Donna and the twins…' She gave a tight smile, as she recalled that Hugh knew about that. 'You get the drift.' She didn't want to go on but Hugh persisted.

'Your dad's getting married again?'

Emily nodded.

'Do you see the twins?'

'Not really. I send them presents and things and they might be there at the wedding but Donna has majority access and…' She shook her head. 'I'm over talking about it.' Emily looked around the staffroom that was emptying as everyone headed back. 'I'd better go…'

It was very possibly her last shift—Emily didn't know if she'd be coming back and if she did she wasn't sure if her notice would be served out here or in Theatre.

It was very possibly the last time she would sit chatting to Hugh.

'I really am sorry for what I said on Friday night…'

'If you'd just told me the truth then it would have been fine.'

'Yeah, well, don't buy me champagne and then demand common sense.'

The opportunity to ask her out was there again.

He could ask her, they both knew it, except Hugh didn't go for a second try. Instead he gave her a thin smile and Emily walked off.

What was it with Emily that had Hugh pondering calling her back and asking her out again?

In that moment he took a very honest inventory of himself and maybe Olivia had been right to be concerned. No, he'd never have cheated but there was something about his feelings for Emily that sat in a place marked unresolved.

There were many women he fancied and he had many women who were friends.

Sometimes the boundaries merged but never more so than they did with Emily. Hugh considered her a friend, though Emily had kept it pretty much at colleague level, yet there was no one he spoke more readily with, no one who got what he was saying even before the sentence had finished...

As for attraction.

Always.

Absolutely.

Yes.

He saw the tension in Emily's shoulders as she headed out of the staffroom and, no, he wasn't going to call her back and make an idiot of himself again.

Emily knew that too.

She'd left things on such a bad note that she'd probably lost her friend anyway if she quit working here, Emily realised. It was a terrible way to end three years of working together, but Hugh would be a very silly reason to stay.

Tears were starting again as she walked back to work but at the last minute she turned around, about to make her way back to the staffroom, but then she saw Alex walking in.

Yes, she did like Hugh in every way.

Maybe this way, maybe if they followed

Hugh's way, she could get the best of both worlds—time with the man who made her heart flutter, safe in the knowledge it would end soon. Maybe it would be easier to get a little bit more involved knowing from the start that they had a use-by date on the box.

She could handle that, surely?

As for sex?

There was an unfamiliar shiver in her stomach as she thought of it. No, it would be a terrible idea and yet…

Emily wasn't completely closed to it either.

No.

If she was going to do this then sex had to stay off the agenda. She was doing this to cement her friendship with Hugh out of work.

A structured timeframe, company at her father's wedding, a few Saturdays shared and then a very neat ending.

And it would be neat because, after today, she might not be back at the hospital.

Yes, it might be nice to have some time with Hugh and then a more natural break-up away from prying eyes, because she doubted she would be working here by then.

She could do that, Emily decided.

She would do that.

Emily walked into the staffroom, out of the corner of her eye she could see Alex at the urn, making a drink, and it would be very easy for Emily to think she had Hugh in the staffroom alone and so she took a deep breath and just made herself say it.

'Hugh, did you manage to speak to Alex?'

She watched as Hugh frowned. 'Speak to Alex about what?'

'Don't tell me you've forgotten! Hugh, you said that you would try—'

It was Alex who interrupted. 'Talk to Alex about what?' Alex said, and Emily jumped as if she hadn't known that he was in the staffroom.

'Oh, sorry.' Emily pretended to fluster. 'I didn't know you were here.'

'What did you want Hugh to ask me about?' Alex persisted, and Emily didn't have to fake being embarrassed as a blush started to spread over her cheeks as she spoke.

'Hugh was going to ask if he could possibly take Friday off and join me for a part of my holiday. I've rented a cottage in Cornwall and I was hoping that Hugh might be able to come for a couple of days.' She turned to Hugh, who was still frowning. 'I'm sorry, Hugh, I know that you didn't want anyone at work to know about us.'

'Are you two…' A huge grin was spreading over Alex's face. So that was the reason for Emily's swollen eyes that morning and Hugh's dark mood, Alex reasoned. Yes, Alex had also heard the rumour through the grapevine about Gina and Hugh getting off with each other over the weekend. 'I didn't realise!'

Neither had Hugh.

In fact, it took a moment for him to work out just what Emily was doing but when it dawned he cleared his throat before answering Alex. 'We were going to try and keep things well away from work at least until Emily started in Accident and Emergency.' Hugh looked at Emily, a wry smile turning the edges of his lips. Well, well, his green eyes said, and Emily returned a small smile.

'That's lovely news,' Alex said. 'And Cornwall is a beautiful part of the world—Jennifer and I have often spoken about buying a holiday house there. I don't see any problem with taking Friday off—we're not on take at the weekend. I'm sure I can manage one day without you. Enjoy yourselves!'

'You're sure?' Hugh checked.

'Absolutely!' Alex nodded. 'I can't wait to see the photos.'

Hugh dragged Emily to one side the very second that he got the chance. 'You do realise I *am* going to have to come and visit you. Alex's son, Jonathan, follows me on Facebook. That's what Alex meant about seeing the photos.'

'Come and visit on one of the days, then.' Emily shrugged, unperturbed, because she'd already thought about that. 'We can take a few selfies and post them. If we change clothes a few times and take pictures of meals and things, we can spread the posts out and pretend that you were there for the whole weekend.'

'We could,' Hugh said, 'but Cornwall's a pretty big day trip from here.'

'Then you'll have to get up very early.' Emily smiled because she knew what he was getting at. 'You *shall* be driving home.'

'So, what made you change your mind?' Hugh asked.

'Guilt about Friday night.' Emily admitted a small part of her reasoning and then she was serious. 'I don't want to lose a friend.'

'You're not going to lose a friend,' Hugh said, and then he looked into her blue eyes and tried to fathom the mystery there. 'I'll never work you out, Emily.'

'No, you won't,' Emily said. 'Anyway, working me out isn't a part of our deal.'

Emily headed back to work, glad that she had their friendship back and very determined to keep it at just that!

CHAPTER FOUR

IN A MINUTE she would get up and get dressed and tidy up a bit before Hugh got here, Emily thought, enjoying the warm sun on her skin.

The weather was blissfully warm and after a long walk on the beach Emily had returned to the small cottage she was renting. She made herself a big glass of iced water filled with slices of cucumber and lemon and headed out to the sundeck to enjoy her latest book, along with the sound of the sea in the background.

Emily lay on her stomach and undid her bikini top to avoid strap marks and settled in to read the morning away. Hugh had just texted to say that he expected to get there at about one and that he was bringing not just lunch but afternoon tea and dessert. The plan was to take loads of photos inside and out and change clothes and things and then Hugh would head off for the night and tomorrow Emily could get on with doing precisely nothing.

She was looking forward to seeing him, though, but was just a little bit nervous too because their friendship had mainly been in the safe confines of theatre walls. It was outside Theatre that things tended to get a little out of hand.

Still, she was nicely nervous at the thought of Hugh joining her and Emily put down her book and allowed herself to indulge in one tiny daydream, or rather one tiny memory, Emily corrected herself as she returned to their near kiss the other night.

Ah, but the next night he'd got off with Gina, Emily reminded herself.

They would be friends with *no* benefits, Emily told herself firmly, and then closed her eyes and got back to thinking about a problem that wasn't named Hugh.

Did she really want to leave her job?

She should be dwelling on that, instead of remembering the feel of his lips on her face, but thinking about work was too complicated for eleven in the morning and she was here to relax after all, so she didn't fight it when her mind slipped to a kiss that had taken place all those years ago…

For Hugh, it had been a long and difficult week. He'd had to take Ernest back to Theatre and was very worried about the elderly man, but he was also concerned about Gina. She had been off sick all week and it had not gone unnoticed by Hugh.

The thought of spending a day with Emily, even if it involved a ten-hour round trip, had been a very pleasant distraction during a trying week. His rare quiet times had been taken up with the question that if he *were* going to join Emily for two nights of sizzling sex and two days of the same, what supplies would he bring?

Instead of stopping at the supermarket for a quiche and a few tomatoes, as well as some champagne, which was Hugh's best attempt at a picnic, he took Alex's advice and rang Fortnum & Mason and ordered their best picnic hamper, filled with delicious treats. As well as that, while picking it up he bought a few extras in the food hall and so, with a gorgeous scent filling the car, by the time he arrived, just a little behind schedule, Hugh was starving.

He had found the cottage easily but there was no smiling Emily opening the door.

It would seem that there was no Emily home.

Maybe she had gone for a walk, Hugh thought, calling out her name as he headed around the side of the cottage to the back garden, and then he saw an Emily he never had before.

There she lay on her back, and her large breasts were, to his discredit, the first thing that Hugh noticed.

They were very pink, as was her stomach.

For a moment there he did consider waking her up by pouring the remains of her jug of water over her but he knew that Emily would loathe that she had been caught in an unguarded moment and she was doing him a huge favour after all. So Hugh resisted a more fun awakening for Emily and headed back to the front of the house and knocked more loudly on the door while calling out her name, and it was that that Emily woke up to.

God!

Emily pulled off that bikini top that had travelled up around her neck and quickly put on a loose T-shirt before opening the door. 'Sorry!' She gave Hugh a wide smile. 'I was on the phone.'

Liar, Hugh thought. 'For a moment there I thought that I had the wrong place, or that maybe you'd decided it was all too much trouble.'

'It's no trouble, if that's what I think it is!' Emily said, her eyes widening when she saw the picnic hamper and then widening more as Hugh unloaded the rest of the car with some very nice treats. 'How much food have you brought?'

'Three days' worth!' Hugh said, putting the basket down on the kitchen table. 'Nothing is too much trouble for you, my love,' he teased. 'We're the talk of the hospital, you know!'

'I do know!'

Since they had announced on Facebook that they were in a relationship the hospital grapevine had gone a little bit wild, but the main comments had been What took the two of you so long? Or About time.

'We'll be old news soon,' Hugh said.

They unloaded the shopping into the kitchen and Emily gave him a little tour of downstairs but halted him as he went to head upstairs.

'Where are you going?'

'Nature's calling.'

'There's a loo downstairs,' Emily said, because she hadn't even made the bed upstairs and she had knickers and bras all over the bathroom.

Why the hell had she fallen asleep?

'How many bedrooms does it have?' Hugh asked. 'Seriously, Emily, that was a very long drive.'

'Two,' Emily said, but didn't offer him the use of the spare one. She had, till he'd arrived, felt a bit guilty about making him drive all the way back tonight, but now she was rather relieved that she had been so firm about it.

He looked tired but there was a certain energy to him, a side to him she didn't really see at work. Usually Hugh wore dark blue scrubs, sometimes she saw him in a suit, but it was the outside-work Hugh that tended to get them into trouble, and now she was starting to see why.

Jeans were just jeans until Hugh decided to wear them. She couldn't help but notice his bum as he put some food, champagne and wine in the fridge. His top was gunmetal grey and possibly, possibly a bit too tight, or rather too tight for Emily's liking because she could see the stretch of lean muscles and when he turned around it confirmed his stomach was deliciously flat.

No, it was the fridge contents that were delicious, Emily told herself as her face burnt under his gaze.

'You're sunburnt,' Hugh said, misreading her flaming cheeks.

'Just a bit.'

'More than just a bit,' Hugh said. 'You're going to be in absolute agony tonight.'

'I shan't, and anyway,' Emily added, deciding to deal with the spare-room issue he had raised, here and now, 'if I am in agony you won't be here to witness it.'

'Then we'd better get started,' Hugh said, regretting her choice but for now accepting it. 'Right, let's kick things off.'

He sat at the kitchen table and pulled out his phone. 'Come and sit on my knee and we'll take a photo of the two of us.'

'Stop it!' Emily started to laugh. 'There's no way that I'm sitting on your knee. Why don't I just take a photo of you and then put it up and you can do the same of me?'

'We're supposed to be a couple,' Hugh pointed out. 'Come on, don't be shy now...' he teased.

It wasn't shyness that was the issue! Emily perched on his knee and tried to deny just how gorgeous he felt to her naked thigh.

'I'm not some pervy uncle,' Hugh said, pulling her higher up his lap, but when his hand met her suntanned, oiled thigh and Emily wriggled to get a little bit more comfortable for the picture, he amended that statement. 'Whoops, maybe I am!'

That made Emily laugh, just enough that a very nice photo was taken and Emily remained on his knee as they examined the image and then Hugh updated his status.

Emily has sunburn in June. he typed, and then, before posting he thought for a moment. 'Should I make a joke about you being a Scottish rose or something?'

'No, because then Alex really would know that we were faking it,' Emily said. 'Just leave it at that.'

Hugh posted his status and very soon a couple of his friends had 'liked' the image.

'We should do a few like that,' Hugh said, but Emily would prefer that they didn't. She was still on his knee and it felt very nice to be there. She could feel the heat of his palm on her thigh and the solidness between his legs and was

actually grateful for the excuse of being sunburnt, because her body felt as if it were on fire.

She smelt of summer—suntan oil, combined
with the crisp scent of her T-shirt and an elu-
sive fragrance that seem to be designed just
for him, because in that moment both were
turned on.

She could feel his eyes burning into the back
of her neck and worried she might leave a damp
patch on his jeans as his hand pressed a little
into her thigh. She was so turned on.

'What's for lunch?' Emily asked, but with the
air so thick and lust-laden even that sounded
suggestive because had he said *This* and then
pulled her a fraction back further onto his lap,
offended was the very last thing Emily would
have been.

Or had he said *This* and then planted his lips
where the pulse in her neck was jumping, Emily
might have found herself turning around and
so, rather quickly, Emily jumped from his lap.

Her T-shirt felt like a blanket. There it was
again—the sudden urge to shed her cloth-

ing that occurred when he was around. Emily opened the fridge and was rather tempted to climb into it, just so that she could have a cool place to hide.

'What do you want for lunch?' Emily said, but her words were very stilted because she was choosing them very carefully.

'I would like,' Hugh answered, equally carefully, because he was as turned on as she was, 'whatever you would like.'

Emily pulled out a bottle of wine.

'That's what got us here in the first place,' Hugh pointed out.

'I'm on holiday,' Emily said, and poured two glasses.

'I've got a very long drive tonight, so I'd better not.'

'It's just for the photos,' Emily said, putting a glass on the table beside him.

'That's very cruel,' Hugh said.

It actually was—he wanted a glass of wine, he wanted to stay here a while, he wanted her to raise her arms so that he could simply strip off her T-shirt.

Sex was in the air and he didn't get how Emily consistently denied it.

Hugh watched as she added a few cubes to her wine. 'That's so wrong!'

'Ah, but it's so nice,' Emily said, taking a sip.

'Get changed,' Hugh said.

'Changed?'

'For *tomorrow's* picnic.'

'Of course.'

Emily ran upstairs and selected denim shorts and a black halterneck, put on some large silver loops and some lipstick then pulled her hair out of her ponytail.

'Wow!' Hugh said, as she came down the stairs. 'I wish I *was* here tomorrow to see you!'

He had changed too but only into a different T-shirt, which was now white and only served to make his eyes more green.

Help!

'Aren't you wearing shorts on your holiday?'

Emily teased, as they headed out to the back garden.

'I don't want you getting too excited, Em.'

He was joking, of course, teasing her too, yet, Emily conceded, he was also telling a bit of the truth. Yes, perhaps the less of Hugh's skin on show the better, Emily thought as she spread a blanket under the shade of a tree.

Hugh was thinking the same because her rather ample breasts were still without a bra and when she bent over, her ample bottom actually had him look away.

'Oh, my,' Emily said, opening the hamper. 'I don't know where to start.'

'I do,' Hugh said, taking out a Scotch egg, 'these taste nothing like you remember them.'

'Have you had one already?' Her eyes accused him of cheating.

'One, when I was collecting the order.'

'Anything else?'

'No.'

She squeezed lemon over wild Scottish salmon and Hugh got straight into the potted lobster, but there was just too much to choose from. From pepper and jalapeno-stuffed olives, to gorgeous cheeses and quince paste, and they chatted and laughed and smacked hands away when someone pounced on a delicacy the other wanted.

They did everything but feed each other and in the end, for safety's sake, Emily lay on her back rather than face him.

'I never want to stop eating,' Emily said.

'Nor me.'

'But I have to,' Emily said, closing her eyes under the lovely weight of feeling full. 'Though the pastries are calling me.'

'We'll have dessert later,' Hugh said, and she thought of the tiny blueberry and lemon-curd tarts and wanted an empty stomach to devour them. 'It will be good for the photos to spread them out a bit...' Hugh's voice trailed off as re-alisation hit.

'Oh!' Emily's eyes snapped open and met Hugh's.

They hadn't taken a single photo.

Which was the whole point of him being here!

'Okay,' Hugh said, and dealt with it immediately. 'Just stay there.' He pulled out his phone and took a photo of Emily half-asleep, surrounded by empty containers. 'I'll put it up tomorrow.'

'And if you write "Feeding time at the zoo is over",' Emily warned, 'we'll be over before we start.'

'I was going to write exactly that.' Hugh smiled but for a second it wavered, not that she'd notice. Emily's eyes were still closed, but because they knew each other so well, shared the same kind of humour, they got all excited over the blood orange no-peel marmalade he'd bought her. The fact that they *got* each other bemused him at times.

Why wouldn't she give them a try?

It was late afternoon and idyllic and more tempting than dessert was Emily's breasts falling a little to the side, her nipples beckoning him, and he moved his gaze to her mouth and wondered what would happen if he simply leant over and kissed her.

She'd kiss him right back.

Emily was very glad that her eyes were closed because she was wondering if sex in a garden was illegal.

Maybe he could stay one night after all?

It would be mean to send him off and there was that lovely champagne he'd bought.

Emily's mind was turning like a carousel as she lay there, wrestling with common sense, telling herself that sex she could handle, it was the emotional part, the inevitable bitter ending that she was attempting to shield herself from.

She knew that his eyes were on her, could almost feel his gaze as a caress, and if she opened her own eyes…

She did and there was his gaze waiting, but when his phone rang Hugh let out a small cuss as Emily let out a sigh of relief. She sat up, glad the moment of madness had been broken before any harm had been done, and started to collect together the picnic things.

'Oh, Alex, hi.' Hugh rolled his eyes as Alex checked in on him. 'Yes, the weather's being very kind. Emily is already sunburnt.'

He glanced over to smile but Emily wasn't looking at him. Instead, she was torturing him with her cleavage as she gathered together the plates.

But then, as Alex told him the reason for his phone call, Hugh stopped thinking rude thoughts and wondered just what the hell he was supposed to do and how on earth he could tell Emily.

'I'll just check if Emily has any plans...' He grimaced as Emily looked up and frowned at him. 'Emily, Alex and Jennifer are heading up this way tomorrow to look at houses and they wondered if they might join us for dinner?'

'That would be lovely!' Emily said, though the smile on her face was black.

'Great,' Hugh said to Alex. 'About six?' Then he gave another wince and ignored her shaking head as he continued. 'Of course you don't need to book anywhere, there's a spare room here.'

'Oh, no!' Emily said the second Hugh ended the call. 'What the hell did you invite them to stay for?'

'I didn't invite them,' Hugh protested. 'Alex practically invited himself. I don't doubt that he's checking up on us. What was I supposed to say?'

Emily picked up the basket and headed back to the house, and when Hugh followed her in she got straight to the point. 'I'm not sharing a bed with you tomorrow night,' she said, because she was having enough trouble keeping them apart with the kitchen table between them.

'Fine. I'll sleep on the floor.' He went to the fridge and finally poured the glass of wine that he'd wanted since Emily had first poured hers.

'You're driving!' Emily reminded him.

'Emily, you surely don't expect me to drive back tonight and then come here again tomorrow.' Before she could answer that, yes, as unreasonable as it was, she expected just that,

Hugh spoke over her. 'If I do that then you'll complain that I left shopping and all the meal preparation to you.' When still she said nothing Hugh let out a sigh. 'All right, I'll see if I can get a bed and breakfast for tonight.'

With a martyred sigh he went back to his phone and started looking for accommodation.

'Did you suggest this to Alex?' Emily asked.

'I swear that I didn't. Alex was actually saying the other day that he was going to make a bit more effort with his marriage.'

'Are they having problems?'

'Why do you jump straight to they must be having problems?' Hugh asked.

'Because isn't that what it usually means?'

'Not in their case. As far as I know, they are very happy, and not by accident.' Hugh added, 'You know how Alex always has a project on the go and he's decided it's time to make it about Jennifer.' Hugh carried on looking through his phone. 'Right, there's a bed and breakfast two doors down from here with a vacancy.' He carried on reading. 'I get a full breakfast served by a very friendly host, which is more than I'll probably get here.' He gave her a wicked smile. 'But I'm taking back the marmalade.'

'No, you're not,' Emily said, and as he went to book his reservation, she gave in. 'Okay, you can have the spare room tonight just so long as you change the sheets and get it ready for Jennifer and Alex tomorrow.'

'Change the sheets?' Hugh frowned. 'I'm only going to be sleeping in it for one night, I don't have the lurgy.' Then he saw her expression. 'Fine, I'll change the sheets.'

Emily did her very best to sulk for the rest of the afternoon but it proved impossible.

It started to rain and so they went shopping in the village for tomorrow's dinner and planned the menu as they went along.

'There's a slow cooker at the cottage,' Emily said as they looked at the meat. 'We could do Greek-style slow-cooked lamb on a nice salad, or is that too easy?'

'Easy sounds good.' Hugh nodded but shook

his head as Emily went to add tzatziki to the trolley. 'I'll make it.'

They got all the usual things for breakfast as well as some amazing bread but Emily was adamant about one thing. 'They're not having my marmalade at breakfast.'

'We'll hide it,' Hugh agreed.

They decided on strawberries soaked in Cointreau and cream for dessert and, yay, they'd found the easiest dinner to prepare in the world.

'We'll have plenty of time to relax,' Hugh said.

'Oh, I intend to,' Emily said, 'but what do I wear?' It was the age-old problem but a real one this late afternoon. 'I packed shorts and shorts and shorts.'

'It's fine,' Hugh said, but when they passed a little boutique Emily wandered in and after a quick look found a dress that might just calm the sunburn that by tomorrow would be raging—it was pale blue and loose and the fabric was so sheer it felt like a sheet of ice as she slipped it over her head in the changing room.

It was gorgeous.

Too gorgeous perhaps for Hugh.

'Emily?' he called from behind the curtain. 'Let's have a look.'

'Oh, you have to approve, do you?' Emily said, slipping it off and pulling on her shorts and top and then stepping out.

'No,' Hugh said, 'I just wanted to see.'

'You'll see tomorrow.'

'I'll get it,' Hugh said.

'No!' Emily said, and then smiled. 'Actually, if I'm playing the part of your tart then I *should* have a clothing allowance.'

It was fun, just fun, no matter how much she tried to sulk.

The shower passed and the sun came back out for its final gasps before it set. They refilled the picnic basket and headed to the beach, and there was no choice but to briefly hold hands as he helped her down the steep cliff path, slippery from the rain, and to their oasis.

The beach was practically empty, a huge

stretch of sand, and the most magnificent sunset was theirs to enjoy.

Yes, it was very difficult to sulk with a mouthful of lemon curd and Hugh making her laugh as they took another photo of the two of them.

'Ooh, that's a good one,' Emily said, taking his phone and looking at Hugh in the image before herself.

'Very good,' Hugh said, looking at the image of Emily instead of himself.

'Send it to my phone and I'll post it.'

'Why don't I just put it up?' Hugh asked.

'Our relationship's starting to look a little one-sided in cyberland.'

'It's pretty one-sided in real life,' Hugh said, but without a trace of bitterness. In fact, he was smiling as he sent the image to her phone and then looked her straight in the eye. 'Or is it?'

Emily didn't appreciate the question—the lust between them was as relentless as the waves and she left his question unanswered as they headed back up the cliff. Hugh, at eye level with her bottom as they made their way up, resisted making a comment about the amazing view.

In fact, he resisted full stop.

The ball had been placed in Emily's court.

Back in the cottage he stretched out on one of the sofas as Emily cracked the champagne. 'God, it's been so good to get away,' Hugh admitted, as Emily lay on the sofa opposite. 'And even better not to have to drive back.' Hugh yawned. 'I've had a shocking week at work. I'm worried about…' He hesitated. His concerns about Gina must remain in his head, but for a second there he'd forgotten that they were pretending. So nice had the day been, he had completely forgotten that Emily didn't actually want him there so there was no way he could tell her about his issues with Gina.

'Worried about what?' Emily pushed.

'Just a patient who isn't doing very well.'

They could have gone to the pub but it was Emily's holiday and all she wanted to do was lounge on the sofa and watch a film.

Unfortunately, the only film that was on turned out to be incredibly sexy and, given that she had already declared there was no way she was watching sport, Emily and Hugh had to suffer their way through it.

'Great choice, Emily,' Hugh groaned during one very steamy scene.

It was torture.

And no less of a torture for Emily to lie in bed a little while later, knowing that he was across the hallway.

Her sunburn *was* agony.

At midnight all she wanted to do was cross the hall and fill the bathroom sink with cold water and drop her breasts into it, except Hugh's bedroom was next to the bathroom and she had the wretched thought of sinking her breasts in his face.

''Night, Emily,' he called out at one in the morning as she returned from getting a drink.

''Night, Hugh.'

It had been an almost perfect day except for

one thing. One thing between her legs that ached perhaps as much as his.

If he made a move, if he called her again…

Just sleep with him, Emily!

But she was truly scared to now.

Today had been amazing and a relationship with Hugh would be very different from the one she'd had with Marcus.

She and Marcus had been more like friends, which was what she was with Hugh, but with Marcus her stomach hadn't had a butterfly house in permanent residence in her stomach whenever he'd been around, and though she'd cared about Marcus she hadn't cared in the dangerous sense.

Emily closed her eyes in the hope sleep would arrive yet as she lay there she thought about the break-up with her ex—the so-called public shaming when he'd got off with Heidi.

How could she explain that she'd actually been happy for him in the end, happy that Marcus had had the guts to go after the love of his life.

Tears slid from closed eyes to the pillow as

she acknowledged to herself that possibly Hugh was that for her.

Emily gave up trying to sleep and took her phone from the bedside table and stared at the picture they'd taken that evening. They looked happy and carefree, which was how she actually felt when he was around.

When he was around, but how would she feel when he was gone?

After her break-up with Marcus, Emily had boxed up his stuff to return to him with much the same emotions as when she took the Christmas tree down. A little sad that it was over but ready to start afresh.

With Hugh it would be agonising and looking at her phone, staring into his green eyes, seeing her smiling face beside his, Emily finally understood the meaning behind a well-known saying.

Don't start what you can't finish.

It would kill her to be finished with Hugh and that was the reason she chose to stay alone tonight.

CHAPTER FIVE

EMILY WOKE THE next morning to the sound of a knock on her door, and Hugh scored no points for good behaviour even though he brought her in a mug of tea.

'Why did you wake me up?' Emily asked.

'It's ten o'clock.'

'But I wanted to lie in.'

'Which is why I waited till ten o'clock. How long do you usually lie in for?'

'I don't have to answer that,' Emily said, taking a sip of tea and wishing he wouldn't sit on the bed.

'The lamb is in the slow cooker and I've made the tzatziki,' Hugh said.

'Did you make any toast with that blood orange no-peel marmalade on it while you were down there?' From beneath the sheet Emily kicked his thigh with her foot.

'Will all my sins be forgiven if I make toast?'

'Nearly all of them.'

He made some for himself too and brought up his own mug of tea. Yesterday they had been too busy avoiding their attraction to each other to spend time working out the nuts and bolts of their charade but agreed to do it now so they wouldn't get things wrong at their little dinner party.

'How long have we been seeing each other?' Hugh asked, as they munched through the nicest toast in the world.

'Well, I said to Louise that we'd been on and off for a couple of months.'

'Okay.' Hugh nodded but then he gave a small wince. 'Have you heard the rumours…?'

'Yes, yes,' Emily dismissed. 'I know that you got off with Gina after the emergency do.'

'But I didn't get off with her. Gina and I are just friends.'

'Friends who just can't keep their hands off each other in the car park.' Emily smirked.

'Emily, there really is nothing between Gina

and I. There never has been.' Hugh hesitated. Again he wanted to tell Emily what was on his mind but in fairness to Gina he couldn't. 'It is going to make things a bit awkward, though. People are going to think that I cheated on you…'

'I'm sure I'll survive.' Emily laughed and Hugh frowned.

'It doesn't bother you?'

'If we actually were an item then, yes, I might want to know the details, but we're not an item and anyway…' Emily started, but then changed her mind. She really didn't want to reveal to Hugh that she was thinking of leaving her job and so people talking about them wasn't going to be an issue for her. 'Don't worry about work for now,' Emily said instead. 'Let's just sort out what we're going to say tonight.'

'Well, I'm guessing that Jennifer might talk about Rima and Matthew's wedding, which is in July. Do you know Rima?'

Emily shook her head.

'I think she got sick just before you started

at The Royal. Okay, Rima and I went to med school together, along with Gina. Matthew's a dentist,' Hugh said as Emily yawned. 'Pay attention, Emily, they're good friends of mine and if we are going out then Alex and Jennifer would expect you to be going to the wedding with me and to at least know a little about them.' He had a sudden thought. 'When is your dad's wedding?'

'The last week of June, but you don't have to come to that.'

'It will look a bit odd if I don't,' Hugh said, as he went through his diary on his phone. 'You'd actually be doing me a favour, Emily. My nephew is getting christened that Sunday and I'm godfather. I think Alex might be a bit more accommodating about me swapping my weekend for your father getting married than my nephew's christening.'

'Alex has got four children of his own,' Emily pointed out. 'I'm sure he'd understand.'

'Ah, but Alex's wife is Jennifer,' Hugh said. 'Keeper of his diary. If it was her nephew, I'd swear that she'd say no, that they couldn't attend unless they swapped weekends...'

'Really?'

'Yep.'

'You can't tell your sister the same?'

'Nope. I actually wrote down all the weekends I was available when she started talking about the christening. She told me she had enough on her own calendar without taking into consideration mine, which is fair enough, I guess, but every couple I know seems to be getting married this summer...' He let out a breath of frustration because his sister was such hard work at times. 'I'm thrilled I'm the baby's godfather, even if I don't know that I'll make a brilliant one, but, hell, one weekend in three I'm on take and Kate thinks it's as easy as swapping a shift as a trainee in a burger bar.'

'Hey, I worked in a burger bar for three years and it's not so easy to change a shift.' She smiled and then frowned. 'Can't you just explain to her—not about the christening, I guess it's too late for that, but for the future?'

'Kate has very sensitive toes,' Hugh sighed, 'and we're not allowed to step on them.'

'Or?' Emily asked.

'Who knows?' Hugh said, and she looked at him because his voice was suddenly serious, but he quickly made it lighter. 'It's no big deal but if you could slip in that your father's getting married, I'd love you for ever—' his smile was genuine then '—which isn't what you want either.'

Even Emily laughed. 'I don't think you're capable of loving anyone for ever.'

There was a conversation to be had but she refused to go there and Hugh said nothing.

He didn't know about for ever, he lived for now. He wanted a chance for them but he refused to beg.

'Am I the reason that you and Olivia broke up?' Emily asked, as they tried to get their stories straight.

Hugh looked at her. She was very possibly the reason all his relationships had broken up.

'Yes.'

'What else would I know about you that I don't know now, if we'd been going out for two months?' Emily asked.

'Not much,' Hugh said after a moment's thought. 'I think we know each other pretty well, or at least you know me. What would I know about you if we had been going out with each other for two months?'

'Nothing that I'd want you to discuss at the dinner table.' Emily smiled. 'I think we're good to go.'

The afternoon flew by. Hugh had, of course, lied about changing the sheets and Emily outed him.

'How can you tell?' he asked, because he thought he'd made the bed really well.

'You just can,' Emily said. 'Don't you love getting in a freshly made bed with clean sheets?' Emily started to blush as that naked thought reared its head again but thankfully Hugh halted himself from suggesting he find out. After all, he didn't want to have to make the bed again.

But *it* was there.

It was there in the kitchen as she whipped the cream for the strawberries that were soaking in Cointreau and Hugh dipped his finger into it and she wanted to be the one to suck that cream off.

It was there in the bathroom as he walked in on Emily putting on her make-up and he got a first glimpse of her pale blue dress, or rather her bare shoulders, and with a quick 'Sorry' Hugh turned and walked out with so much haste he might just as well have walked in on Emily sitting on the toilet.

It was just there.

Which meant that by the time Alex and Jennifer arrived Emily was doing her level best to avoid any physical contact with Hugh and nearly jumped out of her skin when their hands met over the pistachio nuts as they discussed Emily's father's wedding.

'Do you like her?' Jennifer asked. 'Your future stepmother?'

Emily blinked. 'Well, I wouldn't call her my

stepmother,' she admitted, 'given she's not much older than me and…'

Hugh watched as her voice trailed off and Emily changed whatever she was about to say. 'Cathy seems very nice, though I've only met her once. I wasn't expecting Dad to marry again so quickly—he's not one for giving much notice,' Emily said, and then glanced at Hugh. 'Though neither is your sister.'

He was very grateful for the opening. 'Yes, I'm supposed to be godfather to my nephew and it's his christening that weekend but I've already told Kate that I'm working.'

'No, no,' Alex said, 'you should be there for Emily's father's wedding. We can sort something out.'

Hugh followed her into the kitchen and gave a delighted grin. 'How easy was that?'

'I know!' Emily said.

'Though bit more affection wouldn't go amiss,' Hugh said. 'It's a bit strained in there.'

'They might think we've just had a row,' Emily said.

'We're supposed to be dating, not married,' Hugh said. 'You handed me my drink in the same way you pass a scalpel.'

'I don't like public displays of affection,' Emily said, and then pulled a face and changed her voice to a whisper. 'Unlike those two.'

'I know!' Hugh laughed. 'They're all over each other.'

'Tell you what,' Hugh said, as the sound of conversation from the other room stopped, 'Jennifer will come and offer a hand in a moment so if she catches us kissing, your frigid nature at the dining table can be excused.'

'No!'

'Just once,' Hugh said, his hands on her hips. 'Relax, Em, we've done this before.'

His mouth came down on hers and unlike Emily's lips, which were rigid, his were very relaxed and attempting to knead hers into a response.

'I'm not your hairy aunt either,' Hugh said, pulling back, and that moved her mouth into a smile and he kissed her some more.

Sure that any moment now they'd be disturbed, Emily relaxed into it.

She had tried so hard to forget how nice kissing Hugh was.

Now a night and a day of holding back was washed away by the stroke of his tongue.

Come on, Jennifer, Emily thought as his kiss deepened, because she was kissing him back in the way she wanted to.

Any minute now, Jennifer, her mind begged as Hugh pressed her into the bench with his groin and her hands, on instinct, slid down his jeans to the curve of his bum. He could feel the consent in her fingers and then the wrestle as she moved her head back and terminated their kiss, yet their bodies still caressed and thrummed.

He looked at her flushed face and glittering eyes and could not fathom her constant denial of want.

'I don't think we're going to get our audience,' Emily said.

'Do you care?'

Not really.

She wanted more of Hugh. Her reasons for resistance were falling like dominoes and Emily desperately wanted them back.

'We'd better take dinner through.' Emily picked up two plates and Hugh did the same and quickly found out the reason for the silence in the other room.

No, Alex and Jennifer really couldn't keep their hands off each other!

It really was a lovely evening but Emily found it increasingly hard to concentrate on the conversation given that tonight she would be sharing a room with Hugh.

But not a bed.

Emily simply did not want to know just how good they could be.

CHAPTER SIX

'WHERE ARE YOU going?' Hugh asked as Emily, sleepwear in hand, went to head out of the bedroom.

'To get changed in the bathroom.'

'Well, that won't look odd!' he said, with more than a hint of sarcasm. 'Just get changed here. I promise not to look.'

They could hear Jennifer and Alex laughing and talking as they got ready for bed and Emily knew that Hugh was right—it would look odd, her creeping in and out of the bathroom with her clothes, and so Emily started to undress as Hugh lay on the makeshift bed on the floor.

He turned on his side and read through his emails but it was a futile effort because all he could see was the image of Emily yesterday, when he had caught her sunbathing with her top off.

'How's the sunburn?'

'Better,' Emily said, pulling on a pair of pyjama shorts and strappy top and then climbing into bed.

'Do you think they believe us?' Hugh asked, and Emily turned and looked down to where he lay on the floor.

'I don't know,' she admitted in a harsh whisper as she recalled the evening. 'It was a bit strained at times.'

'How could you not know how old I am or when my birthday is?' Hugh asked, referring to a small sticking point in the conversation when Jennifer had said something about it being his birthday next month. 'You came out for drinks on my thirtieth birthday.'

'I did,' Emily said, 'but it's not etched in my memory.'

Actually, Emily had done her level best to forget his thirtieth birthday last year because Hugh had just started seeing Olivia.

Horrible person that she was at times, Emily had loathed seeing him so happy and had been quite convinced that night that Hugh had finally found *the one*. 'Oh, and you didn't tell me the wedding was going to be in the Lake District...'

'Ah, so that was what that dirty look was for,' he said, as Emily turned out the light. 'It will be fun,' Hugh said, 'though hopefully that room at least has a sofa I can sleep on, rather than a stone floor.'

She said nothing.

'Emily?' Hugh said to the darkness a few tense moments later.

'What?'

'I am so uncomfortable.'

'Tough.'

'We could sleep with a pillow between us just in case you can't resist me.'

Emily didn't answer. She actually didn't trust herself to answer because the truth was she probably couldn't resist.

Why was she like this?

Emily stared at the ceiling. She knew why, she did all she could to avoid getting hurt.

'You haven't even worked there for one shift and already you've got all hard,' Hugh moaned.

'Sorry?' Emily said. She hadn't really been paying attention to his words.

'In Accident and Emergency—they breed them tough there.'

Still Emily said nothing.

'Are you looking forward to it, even a little bit?' Hugh asked, because he knew that she had tried to get out of working there.

'I'm not going to be working there.' There was a long stretch of silence as Emily willed herself to open up to him. 'I'm handing in my notice.'

'Emily?'

'I am.' Her voice was thick with suppressed tears because it had been a very difficult decision to make, but the right one, she was sure.

Possibly by consent, Hugh moved from the hard floor and into the bed beside her.

'Why?' he asked, but she didn't answer. 'Emily, it's for three months, it will be over before you know it.'

'Please don't try to talk me out of it.'

'I bloody well will. Accident and Emergency really isn't that bad,' Hugh said. 'Most of it will be bandages and plaster...'

'Hugh.' She turned and faced him. 'They're going to have me in Resus.'

'I don't get what you're so worried about.'

'I'm not worried,' Emily said, 'because I'm not going to be doing it.'

'You'd be great.'

'I'm great already,' Emily said.

'I just don't get it.' Hugh was genuinely bemused, but then Emily often bemused him. 'I thought that you loved your job.'

'I do.'

'And if you want to get on, which I think you do, surely it's worth doing the occasional rotation. From my position it works better—the transition for the patient—'

'I don't want to hear it, Hugh,' Emily said, because she didn't. Miriam was right, Hugh was right—it was better for the patients, and the new system was working well. It was for her own private reasons that she was digging her heels in and she chose then to tell Hugh a little of why.

'You know that sign in Theatre that says no relatives beyond this point?'

'Yes.'

'That's the part of Theatre I like.'

'You prefer your patients unconscious?' Hugh tried to make a joke but was taken aback by her response.

'Yes,' Emily admitted. 'I don't like all the drama of relatives and I actually prefer being in Theatre. I can focus on the patient, I can do my very best for them even if they don't know it.'

'Emily—'

'I don't want to talk about it any more.'

They lay in mutual silence till Hugh broke it.

'Maybe if they heard us at it…'

'Ha-ha,' Emily said.

'Just a few moans would suffice.'

'No.'

'Go on,' Hugh said, and made a low moaning noise.

'Was that it?' Emily said. 'You were very quick!'

Hugh laughed and they lay again in silence and Emily was just about to drift off when another moan came from Hugh, a very different kind.

'Please, no!' Hugh said, and Emily opened her eyes and smothered her laughter with her hand as she realised what Hugh was referring to, because there was a certain regular noise coming from the room across the hall.

'Oh, God!' Hugh said, appalled. 'It's like finding out that your parents do it!'

'Stop it.' Emily was nearly crying from laughter.

'I wish they would.'

It seemed to go on for ever but finally, *finally* the house was quiet and Emily lay there strangely resigned to her fate, because even though they weren't touching she could almost feel his thigh next to hers and if he made a move now, she knew what would happen, knew because she actually ached from resistance.

''Night, Emily.'

A light kiss to her forehead surprised her.

So too did Hugh, rolling to his side so that his back was to her.

And so too, a short while later, did the sound of his breathing surprise her for it told her that he was asleep.

Damn you, Hugh, for behaving!

He did behave.

In fact, Hugh fell asleep with a slightly triumphant smile because he could feel her tension.

Deny it all you like, Emily, he thought as, just before dawn, with its mistress finally sleeping, her body broke from its self-imposed chains and rolled into his and Hugh lay on his back, wondering what the hell went on in that head of hers.

Wondering too what was going on in his own because outside his career Hugh rarely thought in the long term.

He was thinking of it now.

Emily woke just after dawn to the nicest place she had ever been. Warm and relaxed, their limbs were knotted together like the necklaces in her jewellery box…

And she couldn't be bothered to untangle them either.

Neither could she be bothered to untangle her thoughts, because sex was just sex, Emily convinced herself in the rosy pink light of dawn, it didn't mean she was handing over her heart.

A one-morning stand for good behaviour and it had been so hard to be so good.

'They just did it again,' Hugh whispered, as he felt her stir in his arms. 'I don't think I'm going to be able to look at him at breakfast. I'm traumatised.'

He wasn't, especially when Emily opened her eyes and pulled back her head and then smiled.

It was a smile he had never seen and one Emily had never given to anyone before, for it was neither guarded nor sparing.

'Did you sleep?' Hugh asked.

'Not much. How about you?'

'Like a log.'

They were both smiling and she could feel

the goose-bumps rise on her arm as his fingers dusted the top of it and her head went back to his chest and her hand that was on his stomach moved down a little, brushing his flat stomach with her fingers and feeling his breathing halt for a few seconds as she worked her way deliberately down more.

'Not too traumatised,' Emily said, dusting the thick length of his erection.

It could not have been better for Hugh, for he did not want a kiss that got out of hand, he did not want regret, and so her bold decision suited him, as did the fingers slipping in to his hipsters.

Emily lifted her mouth to his and kissed him as she had always wanted to. Deep and intimate, it was a long, silent kiss that had her burn and ache for more of his skin.

'I want this off,' Hugh said, his fingers at her top, 'but I don't want to move your hand.'

'Can't have both,' Emily said, and her hands slid down his hipsters and Hugh sorted out her shorts, both kicking off their bottom halves as Hugh rapidly dealt with her top.

He pulled it and Emily closed her eyes in bliss as he took one hot, burnt nipple and cooled it with his mouth till she whimpered for him to do the same with the other.

'God, Em…' Hugh said, between breasts. He'd known they would be fantastic, they had enthralled him with the way they danced beneath her theatre top and the occasional glimpse of lacy bra, but Hugh was in second heaven and so too was she.

Hugh's fingers were working magic and hers were doing the same to him.

He was back to her mouth but as their lips met again, stupid, stupid necessities attempted to beckon and Hugh tried to remember where he'd taken off his jeans, which held his wallet…

'I'm on the Pill.' She answered his brief distraction and got back to his mouth, but now she had her own thoughts to contend with as she tried to remember if she'd taken it this lazy morning.

Sex, though, was proving a very powerful distraction from bothersome thoughts.

Who cared?

Not they.

'Quietly,' Emily warned.

Face on, he slid inside her and both were just about coming in relief because it had been a very long twenty-four hours, but as they started to move the bed creaked like a rusty gate.

'Shh...' Emily said, but they couldn't stop the noise.

'They won't care...' Hugh said.

'I care!' Emily responded, and a frantic decision was made to head for the floor.

His makeshift bed was actually very comfortable now, because this was no whoops-we-went-too-far sex. Emily was on top and the view really was fantastic now.

Emily didn't do Sunday morning sex. Well, once on Marcus's birthday, poor guy, but she was loving this lazy morning. The feel of cool air on her warm body, the feel of his hands roaming her hips and the dance of her breasts had never found her more free.

His finger on her clitoris had her face redden with imminent pleasure. She almost wanted to slap his hand for it should come with the discretionary warning of flashing lights, so much so that she lost her rhythm but Hugh gave it back to her.

Emily pressed her lips together when she wanted to moan, a hum building in her throat, and Hugh prised open her lips and slipped in his fingers to warn her back to quiet. She sucked on them like a birth aid and then released them, scared she might bite as she started to come. Hugh held her chin up with his free hand, an erotic head support that tightened as his orgasm extended hers, and then he released her. Emily collapsed to his mouth, slowly riding the final waves that brought them both in to a very different shore.

He kissed her for what felt like for ever and then, while they lay there, Hugh pulled the covers down from the bed and covered them.

It was too early to get up and there was no point going back up to the bed, for as they lay in their little fortress, their bodies better acquainted, they both knew from their kisses they were going again.

CHAPTER SEVEN

TWICE?

Emily stood in the shower and let the water run over her.

And she had a feeling Hugh would be more than happy to go for a third time the second Jennifer and Alex left.

He'd said he wanted to hear her moan.

She blew out a breath of laughter as she imagined some version of the *Benny Hill Show* taking place in the cottage as they chased each other around, but her laughter strangled because she wanted to get back to her safe haven.

This time she *had* brought her clothes into the bathroom and would emerge fully dressed and with her make-up on and then get breakfast ready for her guests.

And then see them all off, and she wasn't just thinking about Alex and Jennifer.

Hugh might think, given what had taken place this morning, that the rules had changed, but to Emily it just made her more certain that a relationship with Hugh would be a very foolish thing.

She *was* crazy about him.

Emily massaged conditioner into her hair and she loathed where she was—crazy about someone, that illogical place she'd avoided for more than half of her life.

Oh, it was different, of course, from the other loves in her life.

Dangerously different—for this had the potential for even more hurt.

Back to friends, back to business, Emily told herself as she dried herself off and got dressed.

She tied her hair back and then headed downstairs, where Hugh was making breakfast as he chatted to Alex and Jennifer.

'We've got two places we're hoping to see today,' Jennifer said.

'Three,' Alex said, 'though we'll only be driving past the third one, it hasn't yet come on the market.' He turned and smiled as Emily came in. 'Good morning.'

'Morning,' Emily said. Hugh handed her a mug of tea and she took a seat at the kitchen table.

No, she didn't offer to help Hugh, though she did notice when she went to put marmalade on her toast that he *hadn't* put out her favourite one.

Hugh gave her a wink as she looked up and she gave him a smile but inside she wavered, because it would be so easy to give in, to just fall a bit further into the man who spoke the same language without words.

And then she felt mean.

Hugh laughed when she got up and got out the very, very nice marmalade.

'The things I do to further your career,' Emily said, when Alex and Jennifer had gone and she put the lid on a nearly empty jar.

'I'll buy you a box of them,' Hugh said. 'You should have seen your face when they went for their fourth slices.'

'Scavengers,' Emily said. 'No wonder they

were so hungry!' It was all too nice and too easy to be nice and easy with Hugh so she made herself say it. 'What time are you heading off?'

She saw the slight rise of his eyebrows and knew her message had just been delivered—she wanted him gone, she wanted to get back to her holiday, and what had happened upstairs, well, there it would remain.

'After I've talked some sense into you about work.'

'I wish I hadn't said anything about it.'

'Because you know what you're proposing to do makes no sense. Why don't you at least wait until you've got another job before you hand in your notice? You've got another week before you start to look around. If Accident and Emergency is so bad then you will at least have another job to go to.'

Emily closed her eyes.

'It might take a while to find a job that suits you,' Hugh continued. 'A lot of hospitals rotate their critical care staff. Perhaps you could do some agency work, though you might find yourself pushed out of your comfort zone every shift...'

'Is that what you think? That I don't want to be pushed out of my comfort zone?'

'That's exactly what I think.'

'Well, thanks for the little pep talk.'

'You can't just blow up your career...'

'I'm not,' Emily said, 'I'm just standing my ground. Hugh...' She didn't know how best to explain it. 'I hated A and E when I did my training. I mean, I seriously hated it. I like routine, I like procedure, I don't like all the drama of A and E. I can't stand seeing people so raw and then you're supposed to just...' she didn't know how to explain it '...loan yourself to them.'

'Loan yourself?' Hugh asked. 'What the hell does that mean?'

'I don't know how better—'

'Can I ask?' Hugh interrupted and in his very own way got straight to the point. 'Why did you do nursing, then? If you don't want to see people at their most raw, if you don't want to *loan yourself,* as you call it, why would you do this job?' Emily didn't answer and he looked at her tense lips and knew he was on the right track. 'Or did you always want to be a theatre nurse? Did Emily scrub in for her dolls?' Still she didn't answer. 'I mean, it's a pretty specific goal.'

'I always wanted to be a nurse,' Emily said.

'Then surely—'

'I didn't want to let my parents mess another part of me up,' Emily almost shouted. And she never shouted, she never rowed, yet Hugh seemed to take her to the edge in all areas. 'Hugh, I know myself. I know what I want and what I don't. Don't try and change me.'

'I'm not trying to change you, Emily—I'm trying to understand you.'

'You don't have to understand me.' She didn't want him close enough to understand her and so she asked her question again. 'What time are you heading off?'

'You…you want me gone, don't you?'

'You were supposed to be here for a few hours and it's been two nights.'

Hugh was very unused to being dismissed and given what had taken place that morning he hadn't expected to be so quickly shown the door.

'What about this morning?' Hugh said.

'What about it?' Emily frowned. 'It doesn't change anything.'

'It did for me.' Hugh just looked at the stranger who stood in Emily's shoes, a complete different person from the one who had woken up in his arms. 'Do you know why I didn't try anything last night?' Hugh said, and when Emily didn't answer, he did. 'Because I didn't want you regretting it in the morning.'

'I don't regret it,' Emily said, 'but neither do I want to repeat it. We had sex, Hugh. As you said, being your fake girlfriend comes with the occasional perk.'

'Why does it have to be fake?'

Emily couldn't actually tell him that without breaking down so she gave a brief shrug, and it incensed him enough not to even attempt to argue.

Instead, he gathered his things.

'I'll let you get on with your holiday, then.'

The peace she craved had finally been delivered yet it wasn't so pleasant any more.

She wanted to text him, to ask him to turn the car around and come back. To continue where they'd left off earlier that morning. And then what? A few weeks or months as partners?

The best few weeks and months of her adult life, no doubt.

But then what?

She didn't want to have to get over him. She didn't want to pay the price of love—the potential for pain.

She wasn't scared of the sparks that she and Hugh ignited. She was more scared of the wildfire it would create and the charred remains when it inevitably burnt out.

He had been spot on about her career, though.

Moneywise it would be foolish at best to hand in her notice without securing another job first and he had been right about working for an agency.

A few phone calls to various agencies told Emily that she couldn't be guaranteed full-time

work in Theatre but there was a big demand for
ICU nurses and, with her skills, she could also
work in Emergency.

Hugh was right, she didn't want to move out
of her comfort zone.

She really didn't have a choice and so just over
a week later Emily found herself working in
Emergency.

'You'll soon get used to it,' Lydia, the charge
nurse, said as she showed her around.

Emily didn't want to get used to it. She remembered A nd E well from her training and
even though it was a different hospital the pace
of it hadn't changed.

And the staff still gossiped like crazy.

'So, how long have you been seeing Hugh?'
Gerry, one of the head nurses asked, as Emily
wrote Gina's name on the board.

'A couple of months on and off,' Emily said,
and could feel the smirks behind her because
they'd all heard the rumour that he'd got off
with Gina.

Oh, they were like witches around the cauldron, waiting for the show to begin, and at the end of her first week in the dreaded accident and emergency, they got what they wanted.

Gina and Emily face to face.

'Hannah Bailey.' The paramedics rushed in an elderly lady who had collapsed with chest pain. The other staff were working on a cyclist who had been hit by a car and Emily knew that this patient was hers.

Hannah was gravely ill and Emily took the handover as she connected the chest and ECG leads and Duncan, a resident, came over and examined her.

'Let's get her something for her pain,' Duncan said as he read the ECG, and ordered morphine, which Emily quickly drew up.

'You'll be much more comfortable soon,' Emily said to the elderly lady, and for a little while she was.

'My husband...' Hannah said. 'He'll be worried.'

'We'll take care of that,' Emily said. 'I'll go

and speak to your daughter soon. The paramedics said she came in with you…'

Hannah nodded but even before the monitor started alarming, Duncan told Emily to call for the crash team and just as they started to arrive Hannah went into cardiac arrest.

'What do we have?' Gina came straight to the head of the bed and Emily didn't even look up to acknowledge her as she was busy setting up for Gina to intubate her. As Duncan delivered cardiac massage he gave Gina his findings.

Gina and Emily had worked together for years and, more importantly, worked well together so there was little need for conversation. Emily opened up an endotracheal tube as Gina suctioned the airway and then handed it to her, and in less than a moment the tube was in.

Cardiology had arrived and were reading the ECG that Emily had run off before Hannah had gone into cardiac arrest, and Lydia had come in and taken over from Duncan and was giving chest compressions.

'Did she have any family with her?' Lydia asked.

'A daughter,' Emily said, relaying what the paramedics had told her. 'She's in the interview room.'

'Could you go and speak to her, please, Emily? Let her know that things don't look good at all.'

'Sure,' Emily said, though she would far rather be delivering chest compressions than going in to speak with relatives.

Emily introduced herself to the woman and found out her name was Laura and asked what had happened.

'We were actually on our way here,' Laura explained. 'I'd gone to pick up Mum to take her to visit my dad—he's a patient on ICU. Mum's been so worried about him. We were just ten minutes away from the hospital when suddenly she said she had a pain in her chest. I didn't know whether to just keep on driving or pull over but she started to be sick so I stopped and called an ambulance.'

'You did the right thing,' Emily said, and

then took a breath. 'Your mum's condition deteriorated rapidly when she arrived,' Emily explained. 'She went into cardiac arrest. The doctors are with her now and she's been intubated and they're working on getting her heart started again.'

'What am I going to tell my dad? They were just moving him to a general ward today, she's been so worried about him.' Laura started to cry. 'This is going to kill Dad.'

'What's your father's first name?' Emily asked.

'Ernest.'

'Did he have surgery for bowel cancer?' Emily asked, because she wanted to be sure she had the right patient in mind, and she was sure that she did when Laura nodded.

'He didn't even want to have the operation, he just did it for Mum.'

'I remember your dad,' Emily said. 'I was working in Theatre when he had his operation. He was very keen to know when he'd get a cup of tea.'

Laura actually gave a small laugh. 'That's my dad.' Then she started to cry again. 'I don't know how to tell him. I don't know if he's well enough to come down and see her but he'll want to.'

'Okay.' Emily thought for a moment. 'Let me go and see what's happening with your mum and I'll come back to you soon.'

Hannah's heart was beating again but she was unconscious and the cardiologist was about to go in and speak to the daughter and explain that she didn't have very long to live and that Gina was going to extubate her and let things take their natural course.

'Her husband is a patient on ICU,' Emily explained. 'Apparently he's being moved to a general ward today. Laura, the daughter, thinks he would want to see her.'

Lydia suggested that Emily telephone ICU and explain the situation, and Emily went and did just that.

Though she didn't like to admit it, Emily was actually grateful for the time she'd spent on

ICU because she did understand better how they would deal with this.

Emily spoke to Patrick, the head nurse in ICU. 'Ernest will be shattered,' Patrick said. 'He's already starting to fret that she's not here. Hannah has been here every morning at nine.' There was a small pause. 'Hold on a moment, Emily, I'll just let Hugh know what's happening. He's actually with him now.'

Emily waited for a few moments but instead of Patrick it was Hugh who came to the phone. Apart from a couple of texts and confirmation that they'd both attend Emily's father's wedding and his nephew's christening, they had barely spoken since Cornwall but certainly the state of, or rather their lack of, relationship wasn't the issue now. 'Hi, Emily, it's Hugh. Could I speak to Ernest's daughter?'

'Sure.'

'What's her name?'

'Laura.'

Emily took the phone to Laura and waited

with her as Hugh spoke to her and then the phone was handed back to Emily.

'I'm going to tell Ernest now what's happening,' Hugh said. 'I'm assuming he'll want to see her and if so I'll bring him down, along with one of the ICU nurses to watch him. Is there enough space?'

'Not in Resus but I'll sort out a cubicle for them.'

'Thanks.'

Hugh rang off and Emily took Laura in to see her mother and left her with Lydia as she went to sort out a cubicle and organise it as best she could.

She took out the trolleys that wouldn't be needed and then wheeled Hannah over.

'Dad's coming to see you,' Laura said to her mum, and squeezed her hand. Emily just wanted to cry. Of course death happened in Theatre but Emily did her best to avoid the relative part. Here she couldn't pass it on to anyone.

She looked up when Hugh put his head in the cubicle. 'Is it okay to bring Ernest in?'

'Yes.' Emily nodded and Ernest's trolley was wheeled in. It was heart-breaking because Ernest didn't break down, he just kept holding his wife's hand and kissing her face and telling her how much he loved her and what a wonderful life they'd had together.

'How is she?' Gina came in.

'Comfortable,' Emily said. 'Though her breathing's very rattly.'

'I just want to have a listen to her chest,' Gina said, and she gave Ernest a smile as she gently examined his wife. 'I'll get Hannah something to help make her breathing a little more comfortable.'

Beth, the ICU nurse, said she'd watch both patients and as Emily went to get the drug Gina came over and wrote Hannah up for some more morphine if needed.

To the surprise of a few onlookers Emily gave Gina a smile. 'You've been off sick for a while.'

'I've had the worst flu,' Gina said.

It must have been bad because Gina had lost an awful lot of weight.

'How come you're in A and E?' Gina asked.

'Internal rotation.'

'Oh, that sounds painful,' Gina said, and to the ire of the onlookers Emily laughed.

Then she stopped laughing as Ernest finally broke down and the sound of his tears came from the cubicle.

Hannah had gone.

How, Emily wondered, did everyone but her seem to deal with these things? Beth was all calm and present and had her arm around Laura, Hugh was there with Ernest and Emily just felt like a spare wheel.

A spare wheel with tight lips and tears in her eyes.

'I'm going to miss you so much,' Ernest said, and Beth's arm tightened around Laura as she started to break down. 'I don't want to go home without you being there,' Ernest sobbed.

'I'll take care of you, Dad, you know that.'

And Emily stood there, wondering how everyone did it.

'Ernest,' Hugh finally said when his pager

went off, 'I have to go back to ICU but you stay here with Hannah as long as you need, or as long as you're well enough.' He glanced at Beth, who nodded.

'I'll stay with them,' Beth said, to Emily's relief, and Emily headed out at the same time as Hugh.

'That was awful,' she admitted, and Hugh looked at her.

'It was nice,' Hugh said. 'Sad but nice that they were together.' He glanced up as Gina joined them. 'Hey,' Hugh said. 'It's good to see you back. How are you?'

'Better, though I don't recommend flu as a way to diet,' she added. 'Are you going up to ICU?' Gina asked Hugh, and he nodded. 'I'll walk with you.'

Hugh turned to Emily. 'Thanks for all your help this morning. It was nice that they had some time together.'

It was normal.

As normal as it would have been two weeks ago.

It just didn't feel normal now.

But then Hugh turned around.

'Hey, Emily…' he walked over '…page me when you take a lunch break. If I'm free…'

And, had they been going out, that was exactly what he'd have done.

Emily was about to make an excuse, she really didn't want lunch with Hugh, but he spoke over her when she tried to voice one.

'There's something I'd like to say.'

He *was* free at lunchtime and they found themselves for the first time together in the hospital canteen.

'How are you finding it?' Hugh asked.

'Just as I expected,' Emily said.

'You did really well this morning.'

'I don't know about that.' Emily shrugged. 'Ernest has gone back up to the ward now.'

'Yep, I'm going to check in on him this afternoon.' Hugh got to the reason he had asked her for lunch. 'Look, I never realised how awkward it would be for you and I just wanted to say I'm sorry. I've heard all the rumours flying around about Gina and I and that Saturday night.'

'I'd heard the rumours before I offered,' Emily said. 'They're having a bit of a field day with it in Emergency but I was expecting that. I think they were hoping I'd scratch Gina's eyes out.' She gave Hugh a smile, because when they were together she so easily did. 'It's fun in a way.'

It was far from fun for Hugh but he was glad to see that Emily didn't seem upset about the gossip. 'The thing is…' Hugh stopped and Emily frowned because the usually laid-back Hugh for once looked tense.

'Are you okay?' Emily checked.

'I've got some things on my mind,' Hugh admitted. 'Can you accept that there are some things I can't tell you?'

'Yep.'

And that short answer was the reason he persisted with Emily. Hugh could think of few women who would not ask for more information, few who would not press him to reveal when he'd said that he couldn't.

God, they could be so good.

He watched as she gave a small wave when someone called her name and Hugh glanced over and saw Marcus, Emily's ex, who was lunching with Heidi, who was now his wife.

'How can you be so friendly with your ex?' Hugh asked. 'Olivia ducks into doorways if she sees me and then rings me up crying the same night.'

'Is she still calling you?' Emily said.

'Now and then.'

'Good God!'

'Haven't you ever got upset and rung an ex and begged to give it another go?' He watched as she laughed at the very idea and a small smile played on his lips as another piece of the Emily jigsaw slotted into place.

'Seriously, Em, when Marcus got off with Heidi, weren't you upset?'

'A bit at first,' Emily admitted, 'but then I thought about it and if Marcus was so taken with Heidi that he'd go off for a quickie in the radiology department then clearly he wasn't the guy for me.'

'What if Marcus had wanted a quickie with you in the radiology department?'

Emily laughed again at the very thought. 'Then I'd be the very wrong girl for him.'

Hugh picked up a random piece of the jigsaw and decided to try and see if it fitted, if his theory about Emily was possibly correct. 'I don't believe you.'

'You can believe whatever you want, Hugh.'

There was the Emily who looked him right in the eye and denied them and then there was the Emily he was sure was there beneath.

'Why don't we go to the on-call room now? I've got the key.'

'Not a chance.'

'Come on, Em…' He had never spoken like this to her, but the burn on her cheeks made him push on. 'I am so turned on…'

'Then you've got a problem.' Emily smiled.

'Em…' He took her hand and she went to pull back but then she remembered that to the rest of the canteen they were supposed to be more than friends. Even so, she was the least touchy-feely person she knew!

'I don't hold hands.' Emily went to pull hers back but his grip on her fingers tightened. 'Hugh.' She just looked at him. 'What are you doing? Even if we were together, there is no way I'd…' The ridiculous thing was that his thumb in the palm of her hand seemed to have a direct route to the top of her thighs and she kept having images of being taken against the wall in the on-call room.

This was what he did to her and this was why she didn't want to pursue things.

'I need to get back.'

Hugh just dropped her hand and smiled at a suddenly flustered Emily. 'I'll walk with you.'

She'd have preferred that he didn't but he had a patient in Emergency to see.

'So, we're on for your dad's wedding tomorrow.'

'Yes, I've said that I'm bringing you. Thankfully it's just a small one this time, I was a bridesmaid at the last one.' Emily was actually glad that Hugh was coming with her. She found these things excruciating and at least Hugh always made her laugh and he was doing so now as they passed the on-call room and he nudged her.

'Last chance,' Hugh said.

'No chance!' Emily laughed.

They walked back into A and E and Emily rolled her eyes. 'Back to it.'

Finally he got her words, finally the jigsaw was starting to take shape.

That morning with Emily she had only been on loan to him.

CHAPTER EIGHT

'THIRD TIME LUCKY.'

Hugh turned and looked at Emily as her father delivered the opening line of his wedding speech.

She didn't smile or laugh, as the rest of the room did.

Yes, third time lucky perhaps, Hugh thought, but at what cost?

Cathy, his bride, was around Emily's age and Hugh watched a little while later as Emily smiled and congratulated her father's new wife.

'So when are you due?' Emily asked, when Cathy said how excited she was to be having a baby.

'Christmas!' Cathy beamed and Emily duly smiled back.

He knew that smile well, for it had been used regularly on him.

It was a smile that didn't quite meet her eyes, a smile that, to the untrained in Emily, might look wide, rather than guarded.

He wanted the smile of that morning in the holiday cottage, yet it was gone for now.

'Are you happy for your dad?' Hugh asked, as they danced.

'I don't know,' Emily said. 'I got off that roller-coaster a long time ago.'

'They look happy and it was a really nice service,' Hugh said. 'You really don't cry at weddings, do you?'

'Nope, I save it for the decree nisi.'

'Ah, so cynical, Emily.'

'It means nothing,' Emily said, 'it's just an excuse for a party...'

Hugh shook his head. 'Marriage means a lot to a lot of people.'

'Well, it means nothing to me.'

Emily looked as the twins, her half-brothers, chased each other around the room. Donna hadn't come, of course—apparently she would collect them later. And, of course, her father was too busy to keep a proper eye on them.

She'd cried so many tears over the twins.

There were parts of her heart scattered all across the dance floor and parts of her heart that were absent today too.

She thought about Jessica and, as she did so, Hugh actually felt the tension rip through her body.

'It's my family tomorrow,' Hugh said.

'I bet they're pretty tame compared to my lot.'

'Every family has its things. My sister is the perfect wife and mum but you should have seen her as a teenager!' Hugh rolled his eyes. 'Now she's all butter wouldn't melt in her mouth.'

'How old's the baby?'

'Five months,' Hugh said. 'He freaks me out a bit, he's the absolute image of me…'

'A mini-Hugh.' Emily smiled.

'The twins look like you.'

'I know,' Emily said. 'Come on, let's go and say hello properly, I didn't get a chance to at the registry office.'

They were very cute, very naughty, and Hugh actually winced for Emily when it was clear that they had no idea who she was.

'Can you watch them?' her dad said to Emily when they ran off as she tried to pick one up. 'They're getting into everything.'

Hugh could happily have knocked the groom out for his insensitivity but instead they did their best to police the twins until late in the evening when Donna texted her ex-husband to say that she was in the car outside.

Yes, it was Hugh and Emily who took the terrible two out to the car to where Donna was waiting.

'I was wondering,' Emily attempted, after Donna had strapped them into their seats and was about to get into the car. 'Now that they're a bit older, do you think maybe I could see the twins now and then?'

'Oh, I'm sure you'll see them again,' Donna said with malice that should have been aimed at their father. 'At his *next* wedding.'

As Donna drove off, Emily stood there. She

actually felt like an ATM machine, though not for money.

An ATM machine that had just run out.

'I'm going to say goodbye to Dad and go home.'

'Fair enough,' Hugh said, silently appalled at the way she was treated but knowing it could only make it worse if he pointed it out.

'Or should I stay for a bit longer?' It was the first time he had heard her sound unsure.

'Do what's right for you.'

Home.

Hugh pulled up outside her place and for once he didn't know what to do or say. She was close to tears, he knew, and he guessed, rightly, that she just wanted to get inside.

He'd have loved to be invited in, not just her home but her mind.

'I'll see you tomorrow,' Emily said.

'I'll be here at ten,' Hugh said. 'Emily...' His hand went to her cheek. 'I'm sorry tonight was tough on you.'

'Thanks.' She moved her cheek from his hand. 'I'm going to go in. I'll post some of the wedding photos onto Facebook tomorrow, I'm too tired tonight.'

I get the message, Em, Hugh thought as she walked up the path.

Why couldn't he accept it, though?

Emily let herself into the home that was her haven.

Flat shares had felt as chaotic as her childhood and though the rent was at times a struggle, from the second she had moved in here it had been bliss to have her own space, one room, one wardrobe.

It felt lonely tonight, though.

By her own choosing.

Emily kicked off her shoes and lay on the sofa—tonight had been far better for having Hugh there.

Maybe she should give them a chance?

Just one chance and if it didn't work out she'd survive.

Tomorrow, after the christening of mini-Hugh…

Emily smiled at their conversation, remembering the bliss of dancing and talking with him before the debacle with the twins.

Then she suddenly stopped smiling as she thought of mini-Hughs and tried to do the maths as to when her last period had been.

No.

She was on the Pill.

Lackadaisically, though, Emily thought as she remembered lying in bed, eating toast and sorting out the upcoming weeks, when usually she'd have been up.

Surely one lie-in wasn't going to change both their lives.

CHAPTER NINE

HUGH ARRIVED FIFTEEN minutes early but he held up two coffees so was forgiven.

Emily smiled as she let him in.

'I'm just finishing my make-up.'

'Sure.'

'I've put the photos up on Facebook,' Emily called, as she headed upstairs. 'Have a look and then put a couple of them on yours.'

Hugh didn't peek at her friends or anything, he'd done all that before. He 'shared' a couple of photos but did startle a bit when a friend request from Donna came in.

He was very tempted to decline the witch on Emily's behalf but he breathed his way through it and smiled when Emily came down, her hair worn down, and dressed in suitable Sunday best. 'You look lovely.'

'So do you.' Emily came and looked over his

shoulder and rolled her eyes at the picture of Hugh and herself standing next to the bride and groom. 'Surely Alex must believe us now.'

'You'd think so.'

'Do you think you're going to get the job?'

'I hope so,' Hugh said, 'because if I don't then I'll be resigning.'

'Hugh?'

'Come on, Emily, we've worked together for years, it would be a pretty big vote of no-confidence if he doesn't give it to me.' Hugh realised then he had lost his audience because Emily had seen her message.

'What does she want?' Emily said, then corrected herself. 'Sorry…'

'It's fine. It's just come in. I was wondering the same. Are you going to respond?'

'Why wouldn't I?'

'Er, the way she spoke to you last night, for starters,' Hugh pointed out.

Emily said, 'Hugh, I can't stand Donna, not that she'll ever know it. I'll be friendly and polite if it means I get to see my brothers and I'll be the same with Cathy.' Emily let out a tense breath and then clicked off the computer. 'Yes, I'll friend her but not now. I don't want to think about last night.'

She didn't want to think about any part of last night, especially about the realisation of her late period.

Surely not, Emily told herself on the drive to the church.

Why so sure? the sensible part of her checked.

'Are you okay?' Hugh asked as they pulled up.

'I'm fine.'

'It won't be a long day.'

Billy really was a mini-Hugh!

Blond, long-limbed, he looked as ridiculous in a dress as Hugh would, and Emily smothered a laugh as he nearly head-butted the vicar, while Edward ran amok in the pews.

Hugh did all his godfather duties and he did them well, but as they headed out of the church he let out a breath. 'Remind me not to have children for the next decade.'

Then keep your condoms within arm's reach, Emily was tempted to say, but she knew it wasn't his fault.

The christening party headed to a gorgeous restaurant, where she met his far more normal family and they were all very friendly.

After the meal they cut the cake and Emily watched as Hugh posed for the photos. It was all very low key and casual and over with by three. As they drove home, Emily truly didn't get why Kate couldn't have accommodated Hugh's schedule and they discussed it a bit on the car ride home.

'Is it hard to get a booking at the church?'

'Maybe,' Hugh said. 'Anyway, it's done now, without anyone getting upset.'

'Upset?'

'If I'd not been able to make it or had asked her to move the date.'

'It looks like the two of you get on.'

'We do,' Hugh said. 'Or I think we do…' He knew he wasn't making much sense. 'When I started at medical school I got a phone call to come home.' Hugh carried on driving as he spoke. 'Kate had broken up with her boyfriend and had made an attempt on her life. Thankfully she'd told a friend how she was feeling and she'd gone to check on her. Otherwise...'

'How awful.'

'Do you know the awful part, for me anyway?' Hugh said. 'I always thought we were close. I honestly thought if she was having problems she could talk to me. Thank God she had a friend looking out for her.'

He fell silent. Part of the reason that he looked out for Gina so much and worried so much for her was because of the friend who had saved his sister's life.

'You still worry about her?'

'Not as much now,' Hugh admitted. 'She went very dark after she had Edward but she's done well with Billy and, look, I just have to hope that if there are issues she has someone she can talk to.'

'And maybe learn to say no to her a few times,' Emily nudged.

'Yep, that too.' He turned and gave Emily a brief smile. 'Thanks for being there today.'

'No problem.'

'Well, you've got a week off from pretending about us now as I've got my conference tomorrow, so just the Lake District next weekend,' Hugh said as they pulled up at her home. "Do you want to drive up Friday night?'

'I'm on a late shift.' Emily shook her head. 'Saturday morning would be better.'

Hugh gave a tight smile, because he knew she'd do anything to avoid two nights with him. 'Then, after that, it's my interview with Alex.'

'Are you serious about quitting if you don't get the role?'

'I am,' Hugh said. 'I've already started looking about. There's a position in York that I've applied for. I've got an interview in a fortnight.'

'York?' Emily's heart started to beat faster, not just at the thought of Hugh so far away but if, *if* she was pregnant…

Oh, God.

'If I get another no, I'm gone.' Hugh turned and looked at her then and she was sure he was talking about them.

He was.

'I'll see you on Saturday bright and early,' Hugh said.

'You shall.'

He didn't make a move so Emily let herself out of the car, her heart pounding.

No, he'd said not a word but Emily knew, she simply knew, that Saturday was going to be her very last chance with him.

CHAPTER TEN

AH, DENIAL—SUCH a fleeting friend.

It stayed by Emily's side for the week and encouraged her to buy tampons every time she went shopping till she had quite a stockpile, a sort of build it and it will come, in her bathroom.

It didn't come, though.

And her new friend, Denial, also had a yen for salty peanut butter eaten straight from the jar, which was probably, Denial said, the reason Emily felt sick.

Of course she didn't have to worry, it was the worry that was causing her period to be so late. And don't be ridiculous, Denial said as she climbed on a ladder and stacked shelves on the Friday before the wedding in the Lake District, of course she didn't have to tell Hugh.

There was nothing to tell him anyway.

So why was she hiding in a large cupboard because Hugh had unexpectedly arrived in the department to speak to Alex?

Why was she staring at the pregnancy testing kits and wondering if she should just swipe one and put herself out of her misery?

'Em.' She jumped at the sound of her name, or rather the sound of Hugh saying her name. 'Are you avoiding me?'

'Why would I be avoiding you?' Emily said. 'We're in *lurve*, remember?' She carried on tidying the shelf. 'I thought you had your conference?'

'It finished at lunchtime—I just came by to discuss something with Alex, but he's talking to some relatives.'

'Oh.'

'How was your week?' Hugh asked.

Emily gave a tight smile and wondered how he'd react if she told him it had been mainly spent on period watch. 'It was good,' she answered instead. 'I have a new *friend* called Donna.'

'What did she want?'

'To apologise for what she said on Saturday night.'

'What did you say?' Hugh asked, genuinely impressed that she hadn't told her to get lost but he could feel her volatile mood as she moved pack after pack when there was surely no need. 'Can you get down from that ladder before you answer?'

Emily did so, just to show she was capable of standing without jumping into his arms, but she wanted to so badly. It had been five days since she'd seen him after all. 'I thanked her for her apology and I said that I understood she might be cautious about letting me into the twins' lives but that this particular apple did fall far from the tree and that I'm not going to forget about them.'

'Any response?'

'A lukewarm one but I'll keep chipping away,' Emily said, and went back up her ladder.

Hugh wouldn't.

There would be no more chipping away. She

drove him insane, an obsessive insanity that was going to come to a head tomorrow.

Yes, tomorrow.

He had it all worked out because the contrary Emily was going to be told just how he felt, but not now, not here.

'You're sure you don't want to drive up to-night?'

'I'm sure.'

'Well, be ready at five,' Hugh said, because Emily had refused to make a weekend of it so they were leaving at the crack of dawn. 'I'll pick you up…'

'Actually, I want to drive, my car needs a good run,' Emily said.

'Sure,' Hugh said, and then thought of the bomb she drove. 'Have you got roadside assistance? I don't want to be stuck on the edge of a motorway with you in this mood.'

Hugh watched as she actually laughed.

He'd known she would.

She got him.

Yet she didn't want him?

'Don't be late,' Hugh said, and headed off and left her alone with Denial.

'Go, have a drink, have fun,' Denial said. 'Let Hugh drive.'

But if she was pregnant…

She wanted the excuse of a long drive the next day so she didn't have any champagne because it wouldn't be good for the baby.

If there was a baby.

Emily slipped a pregnancy test card in her pocket.

You don't need it, Denial warned, you'll be caught, Security might be watching you now on the cameras and then the whole hospital might find out that you're *pregnant*.

Finally it was just Emily.

Sitting on the loo as Accident and Emergency carried on doing its thing while she did hers.

She couldn't wait a single second longer and, really, she already knew the answer.

Whose stupid idea had it been to invent a

pregnancy indicator with a smiley face if it came back positive?

Emily certainly wasn't smiling.

She wrapped the indicator in a hand towel to hide it and then threw it in a big yellow bin and headed back out there.

'Hey, Emily…' Hugh was checking an X-ray with Alex and *Daddy* was in patient mode. 'Alex is taking him straight up to Theatre. Could you start getting him ready?'

'I'm just going off duty now, but I'll pass it on.'

'Thanks.'

'Hey, Hugh…' She wasn't going to tell him here, but as two thousand conflicting thoughts circled in her head she did consider that perhaps he should come over tonight but then she immediately changed her mind.

Emily didn't know how she felt herself yet, let alone share the news with Hugh, so she went to the bottom of her list and shared the very last thing that was on her mind. 'Make sure you set your alarm.'

CHAPTER ELEVEN

'WE'RE NOT GOING to get there,' Emily said, glancing at the dashboard. She had picked Hugh up bang on five but roadworks and traffic lights had conspired against them.

Emily hadn't slept much.

Instead, she had lain in bed tossing and turning and trying to somehow get her head around the fact that she was pregnant. Then she had looked at the clock and seen that it was after one in the morning and had lain worried that she'd oversleep.

In the end she had given up even trying to sleep and had just lain there, worried about the future.

Terrified, in fact.

A baby was so far off her agenda that it wasn't even pencilled in at some future stage to consider.

Emily didn't want to be in love with anyone, or anything, didn't want the potential for hurt, and, oh my, a baby was a huge potential for just that.

Of course she had fallen asleep in the end but it felt as if it was ten seconds later that her alarm had gone off, and when she'd arrived at Hugh's he'd come straight out looking so dazzling and ready to go that he might just as well have been on a health farm for a week.

Hugh had taken one look at her and declared that he'd drive, and she'd happily handed over her keys and had dozed most of the way.

Now, though, it was after twelve and the wedding was at one and they needed to get petrol, oh, and tights for her.

'We're not going to have time to check into the hotel,' Hugh said, 'so let's stop at the next service station and get ready and we'll just park at the church.'

It sounded like a plan.

He pulled in and they both got out. 'I'll get

petrol and park over there.' Hugh pointed. 'Don't take your time!'

Emily grabbed her dress, shoes and toiletry bag and made a dash for the ladies.

Her long brown hair she pinned up and then attempted to add some colour to her pale face. Then there was a quick change into her dress.

It was lilac and summery and had fitted perfectly when she had bought it in a sale a couple of weeks ago, but her breasts seemed to have grown an inch on both sides and Emily stared down at the canyon of cleavage.

Oh, well.

She dashed out to the car but then remembered that she needed to buy tights. Out of the corner of her eye she could see Hugh by the car but she pretended she hadn't and raced into the shop.

There wasn't much of a selection and she could just imagine Hugh tapping his fingers.

He was.

'I just need to…' Emily pointed back to the

ladies as she came out of the shop, but Hugh shook his head and gestured for her to come on.

Bloody men, Emily thought, because five minutes was all it took for them to look gorgeous. He was in a dark grey suit and his tie was actually lilac.

'We match!' Hugh said, referring to her dress and his tie, and when she climbed into the passenger seat and put on her belt he glanced at her cleavage. 'Somewhere to put your phone?'

'Ha-ha,' Emily said, as he gunned the car in the hope of getting them to the church on time.

'If we'd driven up last night, as I suggested,' Hugh said, 'this could all have been avoided.'

'Careful,' Emily said, wrestling her legs into tights, 'we're starting to sound like a real couple.'

Hugh gave a half-laugh and then turned and gave her a brief wide-eyed look as she pulled up her tights over her bottom.

'Can I make a suggestion,' Hugh said, 'from someone who knows little about women's fashion? I don't think orange stockings go with what you're wearing.'

'Can I make a suggestion?' Emily responded. 'Just say I look nice and leave it at that.'

Hugh turned and smiled. 'You look nice.'

'So do you,' Emily said.

He did.

Oh God, he looked so, so nice and smelt so, so brilliant and she didn't need rouge now to bring some colour to her cheeks. Instead, she fiddled with the air-conditioner and then looked out the window as they got off the motorway.

'We're going to make it,' Emily said.

'Absolutely,' came Hugh's response. 'There's no way I'd miss this wedding.'

Emily's conscience prickled just a touch because, thanks to her refusal to drive up last night, they almost had. Weddings meant very little to Emily, she had been to many after all. Attending her father's had been more out of duty, and it had been a very long time, if ever, that she had looked forward to a wedding in the way Hugh was.

'We can't park here,' Emily said. 'It's double yellow lines.'

'The bride's already getting out of the car!' Hugh said, deciding he'd just pay the fine for their rather illegal parking, and soon they were in the church and there was just time for a quick flurry of hellos before the ceremony commenced.

'Talk about cutting it fine,' Gina hissed. 'Jennifer and Alex aren't here either.'

'Yes, we are,' Alex said, making his way along the pew. 'Sorry, sorry, running late.'

'I thought you came up last night.' Hugh frowned, because they seemed as flushed and as rushed as he and Emily.

'We did,' Jennifer said. 'We just…'

She didn't elaborate and Emily actually let out a little laugh as Hugh rolled his eyes skywards at her.

'They're like rabbits,' Hugh said into her ear as they all turned round to smile for the bride.

It was, as weddings went, a particularly lovely one.

Rima, Hugh had explained to Emily on the

drive up there, had been at medical school with him but had been diagnosed with cancer just two weeks after she and Matthew had started going out. They'd been through the sickness part already and there was much more to come. Gina teared up as the vows were read out.

So too did Jennifer.

Hugh looked over at Emily, who had that vague smile on that might just as well mean she was watching the Japanese news.

Hugh let out a breath of actual nervousness.

In half an hour or so his secret would be out and he no idea how Emily would react. He had never been able to fully read her. There she sat, under her little pyramid of indifference that only he could see, and he wanted it off, he wanted it gone.

No, he couldn't read her, because Emily was attempting to keep her emotions in check. That was the reason for her blank look, she was doing everything she could to zone out, because never before had a wedding moved her so much.

Confused her even.

She looked at the groom and saw the undeniable love in his eyes, and Rima too, who, despite poor health, seemed to be glowing.

It wasn't just the happy couple, though, that had the rusted cogs in Emily's brain starting to turn. She glanced at Jennifer and Alex, who might as well be confirming their vows, they simply couldn't keep their eyes from each other. Four children on and their love was so real, and she thought too of Ernest and Hannah.

Yes, Hugh was nervous because he cussed when he saw the parking ticket and was unusually tense as they checked in.

There was half an hour or so to kill before the wedding breakfast and possibly a friendship to kill too.

He hoped not.

Hugh really hoped not.

'Do you want to go to the bar?' Gina asked, but Jennifer and Alex declined.

'Jennifer's got a bit of a headache,' Alex explained.

'We haven't taken our bags up yet,' Hugh said, and then wavered.

He did not want Gina at the bar but he wasn't there to police her and, anyway, Hugh had something rather more important on his mind.

They shared the lift up with Alex and Jennifer and made polite small talk, though the lift was fit to burst with sexual tension, and it didn't come from the younger two!

'I'm going to dump these bags and dash out,' Emily said, 'and try and find some stockings that aren't orange!'

'It is so nice to have a weekend without the children,' Jennifer said. 'Nice to be able to have a lie-down.'

When Hugh and Emily stepped out and the lift doors were safely closed, Emily let out a laugh.

'I think Jennifer's use of a headache is different from every other woman's.'

'Do you feign headaches, Em?'

'God, yes,' Emily said, as Hugh opened the door to their hotel room. 'Marcus actually asked me the other week if my migraines had settled down.' She gave Hugh a smirk. 'I don't even get them!'

Yes, Hugh almost punched the air, as his theory was surely proved right.

The more boring the better for Emily.

'Oh!' Emily stared at the champagne and flowers.

'Aren't I romantic?' Hugh said.

'Did you order this?'

'I ordered the one-night escape package.' Hugh took out the receipt from checking in. 'Whoops, I booked the one-night romantic escape package.'

'Well, it's wasted on us,' Emily said. 'Maybe we should swap with Jennifer and Alex…'

Hugh was just about to say it, to admit he hadn't booked the room by mistake, when…and neither would ever know how it happened, but it did. The tension in the lift must have just raced down the corridor behind them and pushed its way under the closed door but she smiled that smile and so did Hugh.

'Oh, Alex, we've got a whole eighteen minutes,' Emily said, and she went for his tie.

'Jennifer,' Hugh said, 'your stockings are making me go blind.'

'Get them off me, Alex!' Emily begged.

It was fun, it was like lovers who had been lovers for ages, just so locked in their new game, getting the other, wanting the other and forgetting about everything else.

God, for the first time since the pregnancy thought had hit, her mind was empty of anything but Hugh.

His kiss was searing, her mouth urgent. It was go straight to bed kissing and Emily had never known feelings like it, never allowed feelings like it.

For Hugh it was like the woman he knew was in there was finally out.

She was on the bed with Hugh standing tearing at her stockings as she wrestled his belt with a 'get out of that suit and into my vagina' feeling but then he spoiled it.

'I booked the room deliberately.'

'Hugh!' *Don't* was the word her voice said.

'I'm crazy about you Emily, and I don't want to fake it.'

'I don't think you could be accused of faking it,' Emily said, trying to make a joke as she went for his erection, but he would not let her sex her way out of it. He undressed and the rapid sex she had suddenly hoped for slipped away at the same time as her dress.

'I only came up with that idea to give us a chance.'

He was over her, kissing her from her neck to her stomach and then down, ever down. 'We've got fifteen minutes, Hugh,' Emily warned.

'We'll be late,' he mumbled into her sex, and she could, if she could just relax, really get to like that, Emily thought as his tongue explored her.

'Hugh, please…' She didn't know if she wanted to pull him up by his hair or push him further into her. Whetted by him, on the edge because of him, she almost sobbed in frustration as that lovely mouth stopped.

'Next time,' Hugh said, because there would be a next time and she'd relax enough to enjoy it, but for now he slid in between still parted legs.

He made love to her slowly and she tried to hold in her moans, even if she didn't have to now, but it was the way he unfurled her that had her clinging onto his shoulders and trying to deny that her body craved this.

'We'll take it slowly,' Hugh said into her ear.

'No longer an option,' Emily said, because she was about to come and from the building thrusts in Hugh, so too was he.

'I meant us,' Hugh said, but he didn't really have time to explain because her mouth was hot on his neck and her nails were digging deep into his back as Emily gave up fighting.

She *was* crazy about him, head over heels with him, every thrust drove her deeper in love and locked her there as he released into her. And all Emily knew was that she wanted this, more of this, as his weight came down on her and for a few breathless moments they lay there.

'We'll take it slowly,' Hugh said. 'I know you've got some trust issues…'

Emily closed her eyes. No, she didn't have trust issues, she had head over heels in love issues.

'We'd better go down.'

Hugh chose not to press for now. After all, they still had tonight.

Did they have to be such good speeches?

Emily sat and listened as she heard about the hard times the couple had already endured and the challenges they had faced.

And had there not been a positive pregnancy test, had they been able to take things slowly, as Hugh had suggested, maybe she could get used to the possibility of a future, a proper one, with Hugh.

Emily closed her eyes for a second, imagining the very free and very sociable Hugh, who wanted to concentrate on his career, suddenly a father.

And she, who didn't even want a baby, suddenly a mum and, no, it wasn't the same challenges as the happy couple that they faced but to Emily it felt unsurmountable.

As they danced she remembered his little dig in the church about not having children for another decade.

Oh, it had been a joke but he was right. Children were hard work at the best of times, and at the worst?

'Do you want a drink?' Hugh offered, as they made their way back to their table but Emily shook her head. She was already sick of sparkling water.

'Have you seen Gina?' Jennifer asked Hugh, as they sat down.

'Maybe she's gone to the loo,' Hugh said.

'She's been gone for ages,' Jennifer said. 'I'll go and check.'

'I'll go,' Hugh said, and Emily frowned.

'To the ladies?'

'She might be outside. She was pretty teary in the service, she and Rima are close…'

Jennifer returned a few minutes later and said

that Hugh was outside talking to Gina. Emily didn't really give it much thought, she was too busy thinking about the baby inside her and the one relationship that might have worked had it not got off to the most difficult start.

She imagined herself up there at her own wedding, six months pregnant, Hugh giving a strained speech and everyone knowing they were marrying because Emily had been bloody late taking her Pill. Or perhaps it would be more a case of slamming car doors, like Donna had on an access visit.

Or Hugh in York and the long, lonely train rides for her child that she herself had endured.

She wanted it over, she wanted away from Hugh, just so she could think.

She wanted to end it and to tell him, if she told him, from the safe distance of cool disdain, and she knew how to end it right now.

Emily knew Hugh's buttons, they had been friends for a very long time after all, and so she took out her phone and pushed one of his buttons now.

Where are you?

I'll explain in a bit…was Hugh's response.

Do you like making a complete fool of me?
For God's sake, Em, I'll explain tonight.

Emily typed back.

Screw you. You've made me a laughing stock
once. You shan't again. Have a nice train ride
home.

Poor Hugh.

He delivered an off-her-face Gina to her hotel
room and then went to his, where an off-her-
head Emily was angrily packing.

'You're not serious?'

'What the hell were you two talking about
that took so long?'

'Emily!' Tonight Hugh might have told her
about Gina, tonight he probably would have,
but it would be absolutely impossible to now.

He simply did not recognise her.

Was this what Emily was like in a relationship, a real one? he asked himself.

No.

He didn't buy it.

'You're being utterly ridiculous and you know it. You can't drive home tonight.'

'Tell them *I've* got a headache and *I'm* having a lie-down—no one turned a hair when it was Jennifer!'

'I'm not telling them anything. I don't have to explain things to them and I shouldn't have to explain myself to you.' Hugh dragged in a breath and told himself to calm down, to try and see things from the irrational side. 'I told you there is nothing going on between Gina and I.'

'So what happened at the emergency do?' Emily pushed.

Hugh just stood there. Yes, he could explain his way out of it but was that how it would be?

Explaining himself every five minutes?

'I thought more of you than that, Em. I thought more of us than that.'

'There never *was* us!' Emily said, and then she couldn't stand to see the hurt in his usually smiling eyes so she zipped her bag closed. 'I'm going.'

'You can have this room. I'll book another.'

'I said I'm going.'

'Maybe check into somewhere else…'

'I'm not your problem, Hugh.'

He gave in then and nodded. 'Will you at least text me when you're home?'

'Sure.'

It was a long, lonely drive back, going over an entirely manufactured row, but at least she had space now and time to think about what she was going to do.

Home, Emily texted just after dawn.

Thanks, came his rapid but brief reply.

Way to go, Emily.

CHAPTER TWELVE

'I'M FINE.' GINA came out of the bathroom and sat on the bed and put her head in her hands as Hugh opened the curtains to the morning.

'You are so far from fine it's not funny.'

'Hugh, I just had too much to drink.'

'Bull!' Hugh was struggling to hold onto his temper. 'I've been through your case and you had a whole lot more than alcohol on board.'

Round in circles they went, Gina denying it, Hugh growing angrier by the minute, though trying to stay calm.

'I can get you into somewhere today.'

'I don't need to go anywhere,' Gina said.

'Gina, talk to me,' Hugh begged. 'I can't help you if you don't talk to me.' It was his sister all over again and Hugh was actually petrified for her.

'I don't need your help,' Gina said. 'I'm going

to get dressed for breakfast…' She pulled her clothes out of her case and her toiletry bag too, and Hugh sat there as she went to the bathroom and then after a few minutes later of frantic searching came out.

'You bastard.'

'Yep.' Hugh stood. 'I'm going to go and pack and then I'll drive you home.'

'What about Emily?'

Hugh said nothing and headed out and walked straight into Lydia, who had a mouth like the Mersey Tunnel.

Great.

Worse, though, was the disappointment in Alex's eyes as Hugh checked out, with Gina sitting in the foyer, waiting for him.

York, here I come, thought Hugh as they waited for the car to be brought around.

Gina slept most of the way and Hugh just drove, his mind in about twenty places.

Yes, maybe Emily deserved an explanation but she'd not even given him a chance.

He was in two minds whether to go round

there once he'd dropped Gina home and explain, as best he could, what had happened before the rumour mill set to work.

Maybe he should but he had been up since five a.m. yesterday and knew he probably wouldn't deliver the best of speeches.

He was still cross with her.

'Will you think about what I've said?' Hugh asked Gina as they pulled up at her house.

'Just leave it, Hugh,' Gina said, slamming the boot closed and marching angrily down her path.

He couldn't, though.

Emily had a new friend.

Hypochondria.

She had got home and fallen asleep straight away, awaking hours later to the sound of her doorbell and a horrible wave of nausea.

It was Hugh, Emily was sure, but there was no way she was letting him see her like this.

Instead, she hunched over the toilet. Nausea

she was starting to get used to but there was also a pain in her stomach.

Stress, Emily said.

It could be an ectopic pregnancy, Hypochondria said.

Er, no, it was in the centre of her stomach.

Appendix, Hypochondria offered, because it can start there and then shift to the right.

Emily ignored the doorbell and went back to bed.

When you were involved with someone you worked with and it broke up, especially as spectacularly as Saturday night, it spread like wildfire.

No one could meet Emily's eyes when she started her shift the next morning and every time she walked into a room or approached a huddle, it either fell silent or they started discussing the weather.

Emily truly could not care less. There were other things to worry about.

Like her ectopic pregnancy.

It was really starting to hurt and maybe she ought to go and speak to Lydia and get herself seen, or go home and see her own GP.

Candy, one of the nurses was pulling some antibiotics up for a patient and checking it with Emily. Candy was sweet and embarrassed and started rambling on about the lovely long summer that they were having.

'I need a hand!' Raymond, the porter, called, and hearing the urgency in his voice Candy nodded to Emily.

'Go.'

Emily raced out to the foyer.

'My wife's bleeding…' a young, very stressed man was shouting, and Emily pulled some gloves from her pocket and went to the car as Raymond came over with a trolley. 'She's pregnant…'

She was very pregnant and also losing a lot of blood.

'What's her name?' Emily asked.

'Sasha.'

'How far along is she?'

'Thirty-eight weeks.'

'Okay…'

Sometimes patients didn't get as far as Maternity, and with the amount of blood Sasha was losing it was an emergency.

Candy was fantastic and even as they were wheeling her in she paged the obstetrician.

'Anton is on his way down.'

'He might want to do a Caesarean here,' Lydia said, rushing in and starting to bring over some theatre packs. 'Emily, go and get the blood warmer.'

Emily retrieved it from the storeroom and met Anton on the way back. 'Why the hell did the paramedics bring her here?' Anton barked as they ran.

'Her husband brought her in.'

All animosity stopped the second he was beside the patient and he could not have been more lovely to her.

'I am going to look after you and your baby,' he said as he examined her. It looked as if they might do an emergency Caesarean here in

Emergency but with Sasha on her left side and oxygen on, the baby seemed to be settling and Anton made his call. 'Let's get her straight up to Theatre. Let them know and page the anaesthetist and blood bank for me.'

'Who's the anaesthetist?' Lydia called.

'Gina,' someone responded, but Anton refuted that.

'She's off this morning. Just page the first on,' he snapped in his less-than-charming way.

They set up the trolley very quickly and Emily did her best to ignore the nausea that would not abate.

She actually felt terrible and as they raced upstairs she did her best to ignore the pain in her stomach, but as soon as Sasha had been safely handed over Emily decided that she was going to sign herself off duty and go home.

'You're in the right place,' Emily said to Sasha. 'You're going to be very well looked after here.'

'I'm so scared…'

'Of course you are,' Emily said, as Rory came in and started setting up. He was her favourite anaesthetist and though she could leave now, Emily chose not to. Instead, she helped Rory as Miriam gave grateful thanks and headed into the theatre to help prepare for the delivery.

Maybe Miriam was right because it was all a lot more seamless for Sasha—she had the same nurse helping her from the moment she had hit A and E till the moment her body shuddered as she went under and Miriam had been freed up to get things ready for the baby, who would be born minutes from now.

Emily should really head back down and tell them that she was going home but the birth was imminent and it felt nice to be back in Theatre. Even in an emergency it was all so controlled and Emily stood, looking through the glass window, as Anton came in and was helped into his gown.

He gloved up and Emily watched as Sasha's stomach was swabbed and Anton rapidly set to work.

There was so much that could go wrong, Emily thought, terrified to be at the beginning of this journey.

There were just so, so many things that could go wrong.

But sometimes, even at the direst of times, everything went right.

The baby was kicking and screaming even as it was handed over to Louise and still Emily stood, looking through the glass, watching as the baby was given the once-over by the paediatrician and then Louise wheeled her out to where Emily stood.

'Isn't she gorgeous?' Louise said, as she wrapped the baby, chatting away. 'I am going to take you out to your daddy very soon!'

'Anton got her out quickly.'

'He's brilliant,' Louise said, then rolled her eyes. 'But I swear he's the most arrogant person to work with.'

'You've changed your tune.'

'Oh, yes,' Louise said, and then looked at Emily. 'Are you okay?'

'You've heard, then.'

'Everyone's heard. God, we all know Hugh fools around, I just never thought he would on you. If it's any consolation, Alex Hadfield's furious with him,' Louise said. 'I mean, he's seriously angry. Hugh is snapping at everyone. Gina's off sick again, which is possibly wise as I don't think she's anyone's favourite person today.'

'I maybe overreacted. I should maybe have—'

'Emily,' Louise interrupted, 'you weren't overreacting. Hugh was seen coming out of her hotel room in the morning.'

And in that moment Emily knew just how much she loved him.

She knew because she didn't panic, or think, *lying bastard.* Instead, her very first thought, her absolute first thought was that there was something wrong with Gina.

He had her love and he had her trust, which was terrifying in itself, but it was the scariest thing in the world to know that she had blown it.

'Are you okay, Emily?' Louise frowned as they walked out with the teeny new life. 'You look awful.' Then she smiled. 'Stupid question, given the weekend you had…' Her voice trailed off as Hugh came out of the staffroom.

Emily would never forget the look he gave her—hurt, disappointed, angry—and she knew that she deserved all three.

He came straight over and Louise left them to it.

'I don't know what time I'll finish here but I'm going to come over tonight and try and address some rumours that are flying around.'

'There's no need.'

'Oh, don't try and fob me off,' Hugh said. 'I *shall* be coming around but don't worry, Emily, it's only to talk. No need to pretend you're tired or have got a headache. We're done.' He gave a shallow, mirthless laugh. 'Well, we never were on, were we? I'll text you when I'm leaving here.'

Her stomach was hurting and her head was all confused and as Emily walked down the corridor those last thirty steps to Emergency looked a very long way off.

'Emily?' It was Raymond who caught her.

'I don't want to be seen here,' Emily said, as she was wheeled into Emergency.

And then she simply didn't care any more. Her stomach hurt so much and there was no relief from being sick.

'It's okay…' Sarah, the registrar, had been called, and she was very, very kind and gentle as Emily kept crying in her confusion.

'I'm pregnant,' Emily explained, 'about four weeks.' Then she remembered that you added two weeks. 'Six weeks,' Emily amended, and started to cry. 'It's ectopic, isn't it?'

'Emily, just lie still and let me examine you.'

It was the most horrible day of her life but Hugh wasn't having much fun either.

He was just checking on a patient in Recovery and his head was pounding.

It had been one helluva weekend, followed by a black Monday.

He'd finally done it.

In writing this time he had put his misgivings about Gina yet there was no sense of relief at doing the right thing whatsoever.

He got a glimmer of that relief, though, just a few minutes later.

'Hugh.' Alex was grim. 'I need to speak to you.'

'Can we discuss the disaster of my weekend well away from this lot?' Hugh said, loudly enough for all the wagging ears to shuffle off.

'It's not about that.' Alex pulled him aside. 'I'm heading down to A and E and you are *not* to join me or follow me down.' Hugh frowned as Alex spoke on. 'I've got a twenty-six-year-old acute abdomen, query ectopic, query appendicitis.' There weren't many other ways to break it and he'd be hearing it on the grapevine soon, Alex knew. Hugh was already sweating before he had said the name. 'It's Emily.'

'Is she definitely pregnant?'

'I'll know more soon. You're to stay here.'

Fat chance of that, Alex thought as he made his way down.

'Emily!' Alex gave her his most professional smile.

It didn't work.

'It's okay,' Alex said, looking at her blood-work.

'It's not,' Emily said, because it would never be okay. 'I'll never be able to look at you again,' Emily said a little while later, with his finger up her bum.

Then Alex rolled her over and gave her a smile. 'You're looking at me now.'

'Hardly.'

He did a very gentle PV exam and felt her tubes and uterus.

'It looks like appendicitis,' he said. 'I'm going to do a quick ultrasound.'

'What about the baby?'

'The baby is very protected and,' he said, 'we'll take very good care, but the last thing we want is your appendix to perforate.' He asked her another question, only this time it wasn't as a doctor. 'Had you told Hugh?'

Emily shook her head. 'I was trying to work out how to.' Then she frowned. 'Does he know?'

'I told him what little I knew because I didn't want him hearing it from someone else. I've told him to wait up in Theatre.' He gave a thin smile at the sound of Hugh's footsteps.

'I don't think Hugh followed my explicit orders!' Alex said to Emily, but for Hugh's benefit too.

'I don't want to see him.'

'Tough,' came a voice from the other side of the curtain.

'So much for patient privacy,' Emily called back.

'I'll get rid of him for you,' Alex said, but Emily shook her head.

'It's fine. I might as well get it over with.' She gave a thin smile as he stepped into the cubicle. 'At least I'll be unconscious soon.'

Alex ignored Hugh when he came in and spoke to Emily instead. 'I'll get you some analgesia and we'll give you some more IV fluids and then we'll get you up to Theatre.' He went through the consent and asked about next of kin.

'I rang my dad but he wasn't there. I've left a message. I don't think he'll come, but if he does, can we not tell him about the pregnancy if at all possible?'

She glanced at Hugh, who met her stare but said nothing.

'What about your mum?' Alex said, and Emily gave a weary nod.

'I'll call her.'

Finally Alex left them to it. Hugh went outside as Emily called her mum but was sent straight to voicemail again.

'I've left a message for her,' Emily said.

'Do you want me to have your phone?' Hugh offered. 'They'll be worried when they get the message.'

Emily handed it over to him.

'How long have you known?' Hugh said.

'Friday night,' Emily said. 'Well, I'd been worried for a week or so before that.'

'And you didn't think to tell me?'

'Of course I thought about telling you,' Emily snapped, and then she was quiet as Lydia came and gave her IV pain control.

Hugh watched as her pupils went to pinpoints

and he put on some nasal prongs as Emily, thanks to some decent pain control, lost her control and told him exactly what she'd been thinking!

'On Friday evening I decided on an abortion; on Friday night I thought I might ring you. On Saturday I had this strange vision of us pushing a baby on a swing, but I had this vision of joint access, and then I decided to just tell you at the wedding, then I decided to move to Scotland and have it and never tell you…'

'Okay, Em,' Hugh said, 'I'm not cross with you for not telling me. I get you were working it out.'

'Are you cross with me, though?' Emily asked, with her own eyes crossed as she tried to focus on him. God, he looked fantastic, he looked amazing. 'Do you think I tried to trap you?'

'Grow up,' Hugh said, but not unkindly. 'Actually, I'm the one who needs to grow up. It does take two.'

'Yeah.'

She wasn't worried about that now. His eyes were the nicest shade of green in the world.

'I'll probably lose it now anyway,' Emily said.

'Probably not,' came Anton's voice, and then Emily knew she really must be pregnant because for once Anton wasn't scowling. In fact, he gave her a nice smile.

'I was just speaking with Alex about your surgery. I'll come and see you afterwards. Do you have any questions?'

'No.'

Hugh did, and he went outside and spoke to Anton for a couple of moments before coming back to Emily.

'We're going to get her ready now,' Lydia said, and Hugh stepped back as they checked her ID and allergies and all the million things they had to before she went under anaesthetic.

And it was then, in that moment, that he got the glimmer he had done the right thing about Gina.

Even if he was wrong, he just couldn't turn a blind eye any more.

And he'd just have to wear it if he was loathed for reporting her.

He could not live with himself if anything happened to a patient.

He looked at Emily and knew it should have been Gina on this morning.

Yes, it sucked big time, but he'd done the right thing.

'Can I have two minutes?' Hugh asked, as Raymond and Lydia arrived to take her up, and he didn't wait for an answer, just shooed everyone out.

'Emily.' He snapped her out of her stupor. 'We'll sort this out.'

'Yeah.'

'I mean it, you're not to worry.'

'I'm not worried…' She put a hand up to his lovely, lovely face and stared into his gorgeous green eyes. 'Give me a kiss for luck.'

'You lush…' Hugh said.

'Please.'

'No,' Hugh said, 'because then you'll accuse me later of taking advantage.' But he kissed his fingers and pressed them to her mouth. 'You'll be fine.'

She would be, Hugh told himself as the hordes then descended.

For Emily it all passed in a bit of a blur. She stared up at the ceiling of a very familiar room. It looked different from this angle.

'We meet again.' Rory smiled. 'I'm fantastic, remember, so you have nothing to worry about.'

'I never said you were fantastic. I tell the patients you're amazing,' Emily said, and then Miriam's face came into focus.

'I'm resigning,' Emily said, as her boss smiled down at her. 'I was going to resign anyway because I hate Accident and Emergency but there's no way I'm going back there now.'

'We'll talk soon.' Miriam continued to smile as a very drugged Emily started to tell her exactly what she thought of internal rotation.

'You'll feel better soon, Emily,' Miriam said, and Emily fought to get across her point.

'You don't…'

Emily didn't finish; she was out for the count.

'Not a happy camper,' Rory said to Miriam.

'It would seem that way.'

A perk of the job was that he was there when she came round in recovery.

'Dad!' Emily was very surprised to see him. She didn't have a clue where she was.

'Mum's on her way,' came a voice, and she could see Alex talking to Hugh.

That's right, she'd had an operation.

Oh, God, she was pregnant.

Maybe.

'We've made sure you get your own room.' Louise drifted into focus as Emily was wheeled down to the ward. 'Give you some privacy.'

There was no such thing as privacy when you worked here, though.

Her mum flew straight down from Scotland and though she was touched that they'd both come it was a terrible strain having both Mum and Dad in the same room, and a huge relief when at eight that night they left.

'Not now,' Emily said a little while later, when Hugh walked in.

'I know,' Hugh said. 'I'm heading home. I just wanted to see that you were okay.'

'Well, I am.'

'Emily—'

'I don't want to talk about it.'

'Fair enough,' Hugh said. 'Here's your phone.'

Hugh walked out and past the cool stares of the ward staff and then to the on-call room, where he'd decided to stay for the night. He knew she'd be okay, he just wanted to be sure.

In a way it was a relief that she didn't want to speak just yet because, though worried, Hugh was still prickling from her accusations the other night.

Then his phone went off and Hugh took a breath before answering it.

Oh, he needed that breath as a stream of expletives met his ear.

'It was you, wasn't it?'

'Gina.' Hugh tried to interrupt and was told

again what a louse he was, how he'd damaged her career, that she'd trusted him.

'Do you know what, Gina?' Hugh said. 'You call me when you want to talk properly, but right now I'm in no mood for your lies. Sort yourself out, or not, it's entirely up to you. Just do it well away from patients.'

CHAPTER THIRTEEN

'I HEAR YOU'RE still vomiting?'

Hugh stood at the door on day three post-op.

'They're keeping me in again tonight.' Emily nodded. She wanted to go home and away from all the eyes and just curl up in a ball and heal, but every couple of hours she started retching and they weren't sure if it was the anaesthetic or morning sickness. So the drip stayed in and apart from a shuffle to the loo and shower she was pretty much still in bed.

'You've lost weight,' Hugh said.

'I was going to say the same thing about you.' He looked haggard and a bit thinner and very, very troubled, even if he was trying to sound upbeat.

'I know it's a shock…'

'Emily…' Hugh tried to keep his patience. 'I've got a lot on my mind at the moment, but can you please get it into your head that I am not cross about the baby, I am not running screaming for the hills…'

'You're not upset?'

'God…' He let out an exasperated sigh. 'I'm pleased.' She blinked when he said it. 'I'm actually pleased that you're pregnant because now, like it or not, we have to talk.'

'So what are you looking so worried about?'

'You,' Hugh said. 'Surgery at six weeks gestation…'

But she knew there was more. 'Hugh?'

'Stuff,' Hugh said. 'I've just got a lot going on. You don't need to hear it.'

'Is Alex angry?'

'Yeah, there's that too.' He turned from the window. 'I'm not exactly his favourite person at the moment.' He came and sat by her bed. 'Your HCG is still rising,' he said, and watched her face to see if the fact her HCG level was still rising, indicating the pregnancy was progressing, might bring a smile to her eyes, but she just stared back at him.

'I asked Alex if I could have an ultrasound,' Emily said. 'It's booked in for nine tomorrow. Maybe when I see for myself...' Emily closed her eyes. It was all numbers at the moment and she could barely remember the brief ultrasound that had been done in Emergency.

'Do you want to come?' she offered.

Hugh nodded. 'When will you be well enough for that row?'

'Are we going to have a row?'

'I assume so,' Hugh said. 'You weren't exactly holding back on Saturday night.'

'Well, it would seem you didn't either,' Emily said. 'I heard you left her room on Sunday morning.'

'I didn't sleep with her.'

'La-la-la-la-la,' Emily said.

'Grow up,' Hugh said, only this time not quite so kindly. 'I'm crazy about you, Emily, and I have been for a very long time, and if you think I slept with Gina after our row, then there's really not much point.' He stood. 'I'm going to go or I'll say something I regret and then I really will be the bastard everyone thinks I am.'

'Hugh—'

'Nope.' He shook his head. 'I can't do this now. I want you to rest and to get better. I'll be here at nine.' Then he changed his mind and revealed a little of what was on his mind. 'Do you know why I respect Alex so much?' he asked. Emily just looked at him. 'Do you remember when Jennifer went into labour and he must have been as worried as hell but he did not miss a beat, he just kept on operating? He knew that Jennifer would be okay without him there. She might not like it, but that was part of their deal…she trusted him. And you don't trust me.'

He looked down at her.

'I am going through some stuff right now that I cannot share with you, especially given the extremely tenuous nature of our relationship, but I will tell you this much. I will do my best to be here tomorrow and at any future appointments, and I take full responsibility for this baby and, whether you like it or not, I will be in this baby's life.'

'From York!' Emily called to his departing back.

'I've already pulled the application.' Hugh turned around. 'Get used to me, Emily, because I won't be keeping in touch with my child via Facebook. Don't ever compare me to *him*.'

Emily lay there after he had gone.

And lay there.

'No vomiting,' the night nurse said. 'That's good.'

Was it, though?

What if the morning sickness had faded because she wasn't pregnant any more?

It was the first time her brain was quiet.

She just stared at the ceiling through a very long night and looked back on the years she had known Hugh.

And then looked ahead to the years possibly with him.

CHAPTER FOURTEEN

HUGH SLEPT FOR about two and half hours and was up at five and at work by seven.

It was the day of his interview but no way was he going to sit through a formality just to be told he was way too immature for such a senior role.

Immature?

He felt about a hundred years old this morning.

There was an email from the head of anaesthetics, asking him to meet at ten, and Hugh wondered if Gina would be present.

Oh, God, he hoped not.

First, though, there was the ultrasound and he was most nervous about that, because for all the HCG was rising, it was a fragile time and again Hugh wondered if he had come down too hard on Emily last night.

Maybe he could put up with it?

Given all she went through with her family, maybe some jealousy and suspicion were to be expected.

'Morning.' Alex was less than effusive in his greeting. 'I want to go up to ICU and check on Mr Hill before we start rounds.'

'Sure,' Hugh said. 'Is it okay if I slip off at nine? Emily's having—'

'I know,' Alex clipped. 'Fine.'

'And at ten I have to meet Mr Eccleston...'

'Mr Eccleston.' Alex frowned, and Hugh debated whether or not to tell him but, no, not just yet. He decided to see how things were panning out before sharing the burden with Alex.

Mr Hill was extremely unstable when they arrived and they were actually considering taking him back to Theatre when Alex glanced at the clock.

'Go,' he said. 'I've got this.'

'Thanks.'

Okay, Hugh thought, making his way down to the surgical unit. Daddy face on? Happy face on? Worried face on?

He stopped at the vending machine at the entrance to the ward and was just buying a bottle of water when he heard his name.

'Hugh?'

Hugh swung around and saw Gina. He was momentarily sideswiped, wondering if she was going to beg him to withdraw his accusations, or plead with him that she was getting help, or just scream at him again. Then he watched her crumple.

'Help me…' She was in his arms and he actually thought in that moment that if he let her go he might never see her again. In fact, he didn't think, he knew. 'I need help, Hugh, now, now, now…'

He pulled her into the patients' lounge and asked an elderly man to please excuse them.

'Help me, don't leave me…' Gina begged.

'I'm not going to leave you.'

'I'm scared.'

'I know.'

'I'm scared what I'm going to do…'

'I'm not leaving you,' Hugh said, and he

looked out of the glass window at the frowning man, who thankfully took his cue and walked away. 'We're going to get you some help.'

He unscrewed the cap of the bottle of water and gave it to Gina then fired off a very quick text. But then saw the water spilling over her face.

'Have you taken anything?'

'No.'

He checked her pulse and her pupils and, no, it would seem she hadn't.

'Help me.'

'I've told you already that I will,' Hugh said. 'Talk to me,' he said, and finally Gina did.

CHAPTER FIFTEEN

JUST AFTER NINE her phone bleeped, indicating a text had come in, and Emily saw that it was from Hugh.

Held up, sorry, I will get there ASAP, let me know.

Hugh wouldn't choose to miss this, Emily knew. He must be stuck with something pretty serious if he couldn't get away for the ultrasound.

She smiled in surprise when Anton came in because she'd been expecting the radiographer, but he gave her a very nice smile back and wished her good morning.

'You're much nicer to your patients than you are to your colleagues,' Emily observed.

'Of course I am.'

She lay back and tried not to let on just how petrified she was.

Emily wanted this baby.

Accident or not, mistake or carelessness, the possibility she might have already lost it before she truly loved it was terrifying.

'You've had lots to drink?'

'Lots,' Emily said.

'So you have,' Anton said as he lifted her gown, because her bladder was full to bursting, which helped get a better image.

Some jelly was squeezed on her abdomen and then came the interminable wait. The screen was visible but Emily just closed her eyes but then she opened them and looked and saw a little flicker on the screen.

'Is that its heartbeat...?'

'It is, and it is all looking good,' Anton said. 'Six weeks...' He peeled off a tissue and handed it to Emily as she started to cry.

'Sorry,' Emily said. 'I didn't realise how scared I was.'

'It is fine to cry.' Anton smiled. 'I'm so pleased it's good news.'

'I didn't even know if I wanted to be pregnant.'

'Well, you know now,' Anton said, and Emily nodded because she did want this baby very much. 'It is normal,' Anton continued, 'especially when the pregnancy is unexpected, to take a while to get used to the idea. How are things with Hugh?'

She was terribly grateful that Anton didn't pretend he hadn't heard all the horrible gossip and she answered him honestly. 'It's a big shock to him too, I guess, but he seems okay about the baby, though *we're* not so okay right now.' She looked at Anton, knew there was nothing he could really say.

Except she didn't know Anton.

Yes, he had heard all the rumours—in fact, he'd just walked past the patients' lounge and had seen Hugh and Gina sitting holding hands in deep conversation.

Anton, more than anyone, knew what was going on.

'I'm going to tell you something.' He actually took Emily's hand. 'I am not friendly with staff, for my own reasons. I loathe gossip and I avoid it as if it were poison.'

'I don't care about gossip,' Emily said.

'Good.' He gave her hand a squeeze. 'Keep your own counsel.'

'I shall.'

'Then you shan't go wrong.' He gave her a smile that had Emily wanting to reach for her phone and text Louise to climb right up that stethoscope, but she restrained herself and decided to put it down to hormones as Anton spoke on. 'Right, from this side of things I can discharge you. Your nausea has gone, the ultrasound is fine. But because of your surgery you shall see me for your antenatal care from now on. Normally it is two weeks off work after an appendectomy but I would like you to take three, perhaps more, and then I want you to come and see me before you go back to work. Have some quality time off and relax.'

'Sounds good.'

Anton left and she was just about to text Hugh *or* go to the loo when the domestic breezed in.

'It's fine,' Emily said, putting on her dressing gown, deciding she'd use the loo on the ward instead of the one in her room.

And then she'd text Hugh.

Nature was seriously calling.

So much so that when she walked past the patients' lounge she barely halted as she saw Hugh. She just stood there for a second as she found out the reason Hugh couldn't be at the ultrasound.

He was deep in conversation with Gina.

And very possibly it wasn't work they were discussing because he was holding her hands.

He glanced up and she could have confirmed the row they'd had on Saturday by sticking up her fingers or huffing off.

She could have ended it then but she kept her own counsel and instead let him into her heart with a small brief smile and then went to the loo.

Back in her room she sent a text.

All looks good, nice heartbeat. Em

She got back three smiley faces and a row of kisses.

And then she got morning tea.

And then lunch.

Then a brief visit from Alex, who examined her abdomen and saw her temperature was on the edge of normal and said he would like her to stay for one more night and that she could go home in the morning if all her observations were within normal ranges.

And there was still no word from Hugh, though it didn't bother her. The less she was told the more important Emily knew it was.

'Em…' She opened her eyes to the sight of Hugh. He wasn't smiling, just looked haggard. 'I'm so sorry I couldn't get there… I'm so pleased the ultrasound went well.'

'Is Gina okay?' Emily asked.

'No.' Hugh shook his head. 'She's very ill indeed.'

Emily watched the haze of tears rise higher

in his eyes and heard him quickly try to grab them back with a sniff.

It didn't work.

'She's in a very dark place,' Hugh admitted, 'but she's finally admitted that there's a problem and she's in the right place to get the help she needs.'

'How long has she been ill?'

'It's been on and off,' Hugh said. 'You remember the first night we got off with each other? I didn't want you to get into the car with Gina.'

'Did you think she'd been drinking?'

'No, I thought she might be on something, or that she'd been drinking. I'd reported her to her boss the previous day. I just couldn't let you get into the car with her and I couldn't properly tell you why. As it turned out, I was wrong. I even had Gina crying on me a week or so later about some bastard who had made terrible accusations. I've just told her today that that bastard was me.'

'Oh, Hugh.'

'It's been a very long day. If I could have been

here I would have but Gina broke down and told me some things that have been going on and how depressed she was and that she needs help...' He looked at Emily. 'You don't leave a seriously depressed anaesthetist alone—can you understand that?'

'I can.'

'I've been worried for weeks. I didn't know whether to speak to Alex, given I'd reported her once and nothing had come of it. I went to Mr Eccleston and, as it turns out, I wasn't the only one. Anton's voiced his concerns rather loudly.'

'Anton!'

Hugh nodded. 'Nothing's happened at work, I believe Gina when she says that, but out of work...' Hugh closed his eyes. 'The lines were starting to blur. Apparently she turned up in the car park the worse for wear on Monday and Anton just took her car keys from her and drove her home and then went and reported her.'

No wonder Anton had been in a filthy mood on Monday, Emily thought.

'How's Gina now?'

'She's been admitted, though not here,' Hugh replied, 'but she's getting the help she needs now. Nothing has ever happened between Gina and I,' Hugh said. 'The world thinks we have an on-off thing, but I'm a very good judge of people and I had her pegged from the first week we started as med students. I love Gina, but not in that way. I care for her and, as I told her today, I will always be her friend, but she has to help herself.'

'God…' Emily lay back on the pillow. He had been so honest. Ought she be? He stopped speaking and looked up as Alex and Jennifer came in.

'Jennifer.' Hugh stood up and smiled at Emily's visitors. 'Alex, nice of you to come by.'

'Ooh, lovely,' Emily said, taking a huge bunch of flowers.

'I just brought Alex in some afternoon tea and he told me some of what's been happening. How are things?' Jennifer said.

'Very well.' Emily smiled.

'Could I have a word, please, Hugh?' Alex asked.

Hugh was stony-faced as they headed out into the corridor. 'I've heard about Gina.' Alex's expression was equally grim. 'You didn't think to discuss it with me?'

'I did think of it,' Hugh said, 'but at the end of the day these are serious accusations and I decided to make the call. I was hoping it would all be a bit more discreet and maybe it would have been if Gina hadn't had her meltdown here.'

'I apologise for jumping to conclusions,' Alex said.

'You weren't the only one...'

It was that Emily had jumped to them that hurt most.

Emily glanced out of the window to where Hugh and Alex were talking, and loathed the mess she'd made of things.

'He got the job.' Jennifer broke into her thoughts.

'Really?'

'It must have been a hard time for him, deciding whether to report her or not. I've known Gina for years. She's the loveliest woman, I don't know where it all went wrong.'

'I guess she's working it out.'

It was an afternoon for visitors and Emily smiled when Miriam came in. 'How are you feeling?'

'Sore but much better,' Emily said, and then she frowned and then she started cringing as vague, hazy memories fought to return. 'Oh, my…did I…?'

'You did,' Miriam said. 'I'm sorry you're so unhappy. I certainly don't want you working somewhere while you're pregnant where you feel miserable. Maybe we can look at you doing a stint in A and E when you come back from maternity leave, or…'

'Miriam.' It was Emily who knew what she wanted now. 'I want to go back to A and E. If I put it off now, it will never happen and I really do want to get on. Also, it's actually not that bad.'

'You're sure?'

Emily nodded. 'It's certainly better for the patients and...' She thought for a moment. 'In many ways I do enjoy it. I never expected to.'

'Well, you've got a couple of weeks off to think about it.'

More than a couple of weeks. This pregnancy was suddenly vital to Emily and after a rocky start she wanted to give it every chance.

'Anton said to take some time off, so I was wondering if I could tag some annual leave onto sick leave.'

'Of course,' Miriam said. 'Take what you need. Then you've got another eight weeks in Emergency and then...' Miriam gave her a lovely smile '...we'll talk about that Clinical Nurse Specialist position that's coming up.'

When Alex and Jennifer had gone, she thought she might get a smile from Hugh and that he would share the news that he'd got the job but instead he wanted to speak about them.

'Emily, maybe I came on too hard. You know I have a thing about women who question my every move, but I can get that maybe you're going to have trust issues. A bit rich, though, given you got off with me when you were seeing Gregory.'

She looked at him and her instincts had been right, they had been that very night they'd first kissed. She simply hadn't followed them.

So she followed them now.

'There was no Greg. I made him up.'

'Sorry?'

'To keep you away.' She took a deep breath and said it. 'I don't have trust issues,' Emily said. 'I manufactured that row on Saturday.'

'You manufactured it?'

'I knew there had to be a reason you were outside, speaking to Gina. I knew you wouldn't do that to me.'

'Why the hell would you make up a row?'

'Because I wanted space away from you to think. I don't want to fall in love so hard it hurts. I don't want to be crazy about someone...'

'You don't want to feel?' Hugh just smiled. 'Oh, dear, Emily, like it or not, you're going to.

You can lock yourself away with boring boy-friends and unconscious patients but about eight months from now you're going to have your heart held hostage for ever by this little one.'

'I know,' Emily said, 'it already is.'

'You do have trust issues…'

'I don't.'

'Yes, you do, because you don't trust me not to try and make it work, but I shall.' He thought about his boss who had taught him so much and the effort he was putting into his own marriage. 'At the first sign of trouble your parents just walk away. Well, that's them and this is me—I'm a very hard worker, Emily, and not just in my career…'

A couple of hours later, her obs done, his pager handed in for the day, it was just the two of them, lying on the bed, watching the news on TV.

'Do you think we'll be like that?' Hugh suddenly asked.

'Like what?'

'Alex and Jennifer. Will you be popping in for some afternoon delight?'

'She was bringing him something to eat.'

'Please,' Hugh scoffed. 'It really affected me that night. I think I'm damaged.' Emily smiled to herself as she turned to Hugh because he still hadn't told her that he'd got the job.

'What did Alex want?'

'A very quick formal interview and then he told me I've got the job.'

'Hugh, that's fantastic. I'm so pleased.'

'I haven't accepted it yet,' Hugh said. 'I said I needed to speak to you first.'

'Speak to me?'

'I don't know if you'd prefer a fresh start,' Hugh said. 'We do have a bit of history scattered around the hospital.'

'Er, I have one bit of history,' Emily said, referring to Marcus.

'Exactly,' Hugh said. 'And I get it if you want to make a go of things well away from my past.'

'There's no need,' Emily said.

'You're sure?'

'Absolutely.' She turned to him. 'I'm sorry. I don't know how you put up with me...'

'I have asked myself that a few times,' Hugh admitted.

'But you did?'

'Yep, I told you—I work at things.'

'But—'

'I love you,' Hugh said, as if it was the least complicated emotion in the world, and maybe sometimes it was because it was right here in the room. 'Whenever you're ready, Emily,' he nudged.

'Iloveyoutoo.' She said it very quickly, more as one word, but Hugh just smiled.

'Progress!'

Emily reached for her phone. 'I'd better call Dad and let him know I'll definitely be home tomorrow. He and my new stepmum are going to come over and then Mum will come down...'

'You really don't get this partnership lark, do you?' Hugh said. 'Ring your father and tell him there's no need to worry. I've got five days' carer's leave.'

'Oh!'

'Alex told me. Well, so long as we're living together...' He gave her a very nice smile. 'Your place or mine?' Hugh said.

'Mine,' Emily said, because she wanted to recover among her own things, wanted her own bed, her own bathroom. And then she looked at Hugh and amended all that, because more than that she wanted him. 'To pick up a few things.'

'Good choice,' Hugh said, 'because I have a cleaner who comes in every other day.'

'Ooh!' Emily smiled. 'How lovely.'

The future suddenly was.

CHAPTER SIXTEEN

EMILY DID PICK up a few things and on her second trip Hugh asked that she pick up a few more things, namely her birth certificate.

Which she did.

But staring at the mountain of paperwork, just thinking of the impossibility of it all, Emily baulked at the final moment.

'I don't want to get married, Hugh.'

'It will be tiny,' Hugh said. They'd *almost* decided to get married in Scotland at her old church but just the thought of her mum and her dad and half-brothers and -sisters and even Jessica, who was now a Facebook friend, tiny was something it could never be.

'I don't want to,' Emily said. 'You said we could take things slowly.'

'That was before I knew you were pregnant,' Hugh said, but then dropped it.

'Will you be all right tomorrow?' Hugh checked, because after a weekend off and five days' leave he was back at work and on call for the entire weekend. 'Your mum said she'd come down and Kate's going to drop in.'

'Hugh, I don't need anyone. I'm not even sore now.'

Just tired.

Kate did drop in and so too did her dad, and he brought the twins, who were on a weekend access. And then Jessica sent her a message and asked if she could drop by, which she did.

'These are for you,' Jessica said, handing over some DVDs. It was the entire series of a show Emily had said in passing during their chats that she'd never watched. 'Well, when I say they're for you I want them back, but I watched them back to back after I had my operation.'

It was funny but after all these years apart they slipped back so easily and Jessica set up the DVD in Hugh's bedroom and they watched the first episode together and then the second.

'One more,' Emily said, only pausing it to

take a call from her mum, who felt a little put out that Emily hadn't needed her to come down.

'Mum's coming next week with Abby,' Emily said as she concluded the call. 'It's exhausting, being sick.'

It was nice, though.

Not the surgery part but finally, after all these years, Emily knew she had a family. As complicated as it was, as scattered as they were, the news about her operation had somehow reminded people about the relative that they'd tended to forget, and finally Emily knew she was loved. The twins now knew who she was and Emily was determined that it would remain that way.

Best of all, though, was knowing she had Hugh and also knowing that he had her.

'What happened to the bedroom?' Hugh asked, when he came home a little grey around the gills after a long weekend on call, but he had stopped for two coffees on the way and handed her one as he looked around the room. The television was at the foot of the bed and it looked like there had been a little party and there sat Emily in bed, having pressed the pause button on her show at the sound of his car.

It was very nice to come home to.

'Jessica set up the room,' Emily said, taking a long drink of coffee. 'Is that okay?'

'Of course,' Hugh said. 'I should have thought to bring the television down.'

'I'm fine,' Emily said. 'I was just being a sloth. It was so good. How was work?'

'Busy,' Hugh said, 'but good. At least till this morning.' He pulled a face. 'Ernest Bailey died in the small hours.'

'I'm sorry,' Emily said. 'Was it expected?'

'Nope.' Hugh shook his head and told her what had happened as he got undressed. 'He was supposed to be discharged home this morning. He was going to live with his daughter.' Hugh had a quick shower and then, damp and lovely, he climbed into bed. 'He didn't really want to go and live with his daughter. He was a very proud man. He couldn't have lived alone, though.' Hugh lay and thought for a moment. 'I spoke with Laura for a long time and she said it's how he would have wanted it.'

'Did he get his cup of tea?'

'Many of them. Laura brought a Thermos in for him to have by his bed every night.' Hugh was quiet for a moment. 'I had a little cry but then I knew she was right—it would have been their golden wedding anniversary tomorrow, so it's nice that they're together.'

She looked at Hugh and he looked back and smiled. 'I didn't boo-hoo.'

'I know.'

'I've got to go to sleep.'

'So do I,' Emily said. 'I'm on Hugh time. I've been up all night. One more episode to go.'

'Watch it now.'

'No, no, I'll save it for tonight.'

'Just watch it. You know you want to.'

Did life get better than this? Emily wondered as her back-to-back DVD marathon concluded. Hugh was half-asleep beside her and the last sip of coffee was still warm as she flicked off the television.

'Was it good?' Hugh asked, pulling her down beside him.

'So good,' Emily said. 'I've never done that before—watched a whole series back to back.'

'It's the best way,' Hugh mumbled. 'I've been thinking...' He had. Hugh had been lying there thinking of Ernest and Hannah and all the things that mattered most. 'After you see Anton for your check-up I've got a long weekend. Do you want to go to the Lake District? Maybe take a few days before you go back to work?'

'I'd love to.'

'We never did get full use of that room.'

'It would be lovely,' Emily said. 'Go to sleep.'

They had a kiss and she felt his hair in her hands still damp from the shower and she revelled in his sleepy kiss. Emily changed her mind—about sleeping, that was—because her other hand moved down his torso, their kiss moving seamlessly from tender to passionate by the swirl of her tongue. She loved the quickening of his breath and how he gathered her closer into him. There was no need to ask if it was too soon, or if she was ready, her body just was. Warm and relaxed and turned on in his arms, the icing appeared on the cake as Hugh kissed her till she lay beneath him and he took all his weight on his elbows. 'I missed you,' Hugh said.

She had missed him too but was just a little nervous as he entered her, scared that something might tear, but he took it really slowly and gave her time to get accustomed to the stretch of him inside her, and then slowly, as he moved inside her, her abdomen learned how first to relax and then it started to tense, but in pleasure now.

Emily's hands met behind his neck, loving the sight of his concentrated effort and the pleasure that was moving through her, the delicious friction combined with tenderness, and this risky thing called love that came with benefits galore.

She could feel his restraint and it turned her on, could feel him holding back from driving in deep, and as his arm slipped under her back and lifted her higher into him, it possibly hurt a bit but she'd take it for the pleasure as her orgasm started to home in and, yes, she was ready, more than ready as Hugh started to thrust faster while holding back on going very deep. One final swell of Hugh and then the bliss of his release gave him two gifts—a liberating shout of pleasure from Emily, combined with a very intense orgasm. They both welcomed the rewards of his restraint.

'I'll sleep now,' Hugh said, smiling down at her. 'Can we pretend you've just had surgery quite often?'

'We can.' Emily smiled.

'Depending on your migraines, of course.'

'I don't get migraines any more.' It was lovely to smile at their history, to lie and fall asleep in each other's arms and know they were the person the other wanted beside them in everything yet to come.

Yes, Emily thought as she drifted off to sleep, life could not get better than this.

She was wrong.

CHAPTER SEVENTEEN

'I CAN COME with you if Hugh can't make it,' Louise offered.

Emily had just seen Alex for her post-operative check-up and was having a coffee up in Theatre before her antenatal appointment with Anton.

'I'll be fine.' Emily smiled. 'And you were right, he is lovely to his patients.'

'Told you,' Louise said. 'Shame he's so miserable with all the staff. Honestly, I am so tired of him checking and re-checking everything. I wonder what he's like with the staff on Maternity.'

'You'll find out soon,' Emily said, because Louise was starting there next week. 'I'm sorry I can't make your leaving do. Hugh had already booked for us to go to the Lake District before I knew the date.'

'It's fine,' Louise said. 'I'm sure there'll be other nights out. You'd better head down for your appointment. You don't want to keep Anton waiting.'

Emily walked from Theatre down to Maternity Outpatients and tried to tell herself that it was natural to be nervous.

It didn't worry her that Hugh hadn't made it, but then she saw him walking briskly toward her and it was very, very nice that he had.

Emily gave her name at Reception and then they took their seats to wait their turn to see Anton.

'Why don't we drive tomorrow?' Emily said, but Hugh shook his head.

'I'm going to have a sleep when we get in and then we can head off at midnight. I've only got four days off.'

And Hugh wanted to squeeze everything in.

'Are you nervous?'

'Yes,' Emily admitted. 'You?'

'Yes,' Hugh said, though he actually wasn't too nervous about the appointment. He had an awful lot else to be nervous about, though he daren't tell Emily just yet.

'Good to see they keep doctors waiting too,' Hugh said, and she pulled a face.

'I'm a nurse and this is my appointment.'

It was Hugh who smiled now. They knew just how to wind the other up, just how to make the other smile. Living together was a journey of both discovery and also a kind familiarity. They had been friends for way longer than they should have been after all.

'Well, if I was pregnant,' Hugh said, 'I'd expect to be seen on time.'

'If you were pregnant, you'd be seen on time by every doctor and medical student in the place.'

It was a very long wait and Hugh tapped his feet with impatience and read all the sex tips in all the magazines, along with the problem pages, as Emily read her book and tried to tell herself it would all be fine.

'Emily Jackson.'

Finally they were called in.

'Get used to waiting.' Anton smiled by way of greeting. 'One day it might be you two keeping the waiting room waiting.'

'Might be?' Emily checked, as he took her blood pressure.

'Planned Caesareans, for me, are a very beautiful thing.' Anton smiled again and Emily blushed. Louise was right, he was gorgeous. Oh, God, she was going to be one of those women who had a crush on their obstetrician. How embarrassing!

They went through all the usual questions and he asked if she had any plans for her delivery.

'None,' Emily said.

'Are you still getting used to the idea that you're pregnant?'

'I'm used to it being in there now,' Emily said. 'I've just not thought as far as getting it out.'

'Well, you're not due till the twenty fourth of February so you have plenty of time to work out your birth plan.'

'Lots of drugs,' Emily said, recalling the screams that had come from Theatre. 'Actually, that planned Caesarean is starting to sound very beautiful to me too.'

Anton continued smiling. 'Let's see how things progress. Usually I don't do an ultrasound at this stage,' Anton said, 'but I would like to just check and I'm sure you want to see for yourself that it is all okay, and then we can leave things till the nineteen-week scan.'

Hugh hadn't been there for her ultrasound and he saw their baby for the very first time. There was a lot more to see four weeks later and it moved and wriggled and Hugh could barely take in the evidence of what had happened that morning.

'Meant to be,' Hugh said.

It was.

As they headed off for a mountain of blood tests, she realised again that Hugh knew her very well indeed. 'You fancy him, don't you?'

'Stop it.' Emily was appalled that he could tell. 'Maybe it's hormones.'

'Or that Italian accent,' Hugh nudged, and then stopped teasing. 'I'm sure he's very used to his patients being a little in love with him. Apparently he's got a very good success rate for IVF. He was a top fertility specialist in Milan. It would seem you're in very good hands.'

Emily had her bloods done and then booked in for her nineteen-week ultrasound. 'We're not finding out what we're having,' Emily said, because Hugh wanted to and she didn't.

'Fine.'

'And if you can tell from the ultrasound then please don't tell me.'

'I'm not going to,' Hugh said, and then gave her a warning of how it would be. 'No matter how many times you ask me.'

Emily smiled. There was a lot to smile about, but not when Hugh woke her up at midnight and said that it was time to head off.

'Can't we drive in the morning?'

'No,' Hugh said. 'I want to be there by morning.'

It was actually nice, driving through the darkness and chatting away, and Emily asked if he'd heard any more about Gina.

'I'll go and visit next week,' Hugh said, 'but Mr Eccleston went and saw her yesterday and she's doing very well apparently. Her family hasn't exactly rallied around her though. She wants to get out of anaesthetics.' He glanced at her. 'Why don't you go to sleep?'

'Isn't the passenger supposed to talk to keep the driver awake?'

'You've never bothered before,' Hugh pointed out. 'Have a sleep. I'm fine, I had a few hours when we got home.'

Emily dozed off just before dawn, thinking about Gina and all the decisions she had to make but so glad she was getting help and support. She awoke a couple of hours later, frowning when she saw the road signs for Carlisle and trying to orientate herself for they'd passed the exit for the Lake District.

'We've passed it.'

'I know.'

'Shouldn't we—?'

'We're not going to the Lake District,' Hugh said. 'We're eloping.'

'Sorry?'

'We're going to Gretna Green. Remember those forms you signed…'

'And remember that I then changed my mind,' Emily reminded him. 'Hugh, I told you, it doesn't mean anything.'

'Well, it does to me. Even if your parents don't take their vows seriously, I will, and I believe you will too. I'm not going to force you but, honestly, if it really means nothing to you, do it for me.' Emily sat there. 'I don't want to hear them call out Ms Jackson. I don't want our baby to be called Jackson-Linton or Linton-Jackson. Boring as I am, I want us all to have the same surname. Now, if marriage does mean something to you and you don't think I'm the man you want to marry then it's a different story…'

'You are the one.' She did want to be married, she was just scared. 'I just swore I never would.'

'If this marriage doesn't work,' Hugh said, 'I won't be doing it again. I'm not going to have our child walking up the aisle behind one of its parents over and over… We'll do it once,' Hugh said. 'That can be our vow.'

'What if—?'

'Widow and widowers excepted.' Hugh smiled. 'I'll leave you rich enough to be a very wicked widow.' Then he was serious. 'Marry me, Emily.'

She nodded.

'Is that a yes?'

'Yes, but so many people are going to be upset…' Emily stopped there and then. She didn't care if her marriage offended some people, for their efforts had offended her deeply after all, but then she thought of something. 'Won't your parents be upset?'

'They were a bit at first.'

'You've already told them?'

'Yes.' Hugh nodded. 'Then Kate came up with a plan that they'd all book into a hotel and if you said yes…' Hugh shook his head. 'No way!'

'You said no to her.'

'We had a row actually,' Hugh said, 'and, God, it felt good. I said that I didn't even know if you were going to say yes. I didn't want complete public humiliation.'

'Oh, Hugh.' She couldn't believe all he'd been through just to get her to this point and, no, she couldn't say no to him.

'I'd love to marry you,' Emily said. 'And, for the record, it means everything to me.'

'We get married at three,' Hugh said, as the signs came up for Gretna Green.

'What about—?'

'I've covered everything.' He gave her a very nice smile. 'Don't panic, I have very good taste and once Kate had got over her hissy fit she actually helped me with a lot of the arrangements.'

They stopped thirty minutes from Gretna Green to pick up the rings that Hugh had chosen—Emily's a diamond and platinum ring stamped with an image of the anvil. It could not have been a better choice. And Hugh's ring was the same, just minus the diamonds.

'So you don't say I cheated you out of an engagement ring,' Hugh explained.

Emily's nerves were really fluttering as they

pulled up at a small hotel and Hugh told her he'd booked her in for hair and make-up, which was all very lovely but there was nothing in her case for such a big day.

'God, what do I wear?'

He *had* thought of everything.

Hugh opened his suitcase and there, wrapped in tissue paper, was an ivory dress.

'You know your favourite black dress, the one you said ages ago that you wish you'd bought it in every size, because it was perfect for you?'

That conversation had been close to two years ago and that he'd remembered, that he knew it was still her favourite dress touched Emily deeply. 'I had it made up…'

'You've really planned this.'

'Oh, yes,' Hugh said. 'Now, are you sure you don't want to ring your parents? We can delay it.'

'No.'

'Do you want Louise or—?'

'I just want you, Hugh.' Now she could more easily admit it. 'I always have.'

'Then let's make it official.'

It was the only way Emily could have ever married, or rather the best way for Emily to marry, and it was the most beautiful day, apart from her feet, because a half-size up would have been better but she chose not to say anything.

It was near the end of summer and the beginning of their new lives.

A piper walked Emily to the wedding room and Hugh was wrong about one thing.

She did cry at weddings.

But only her own.

Emily looked down as he slid a ring on her finger and they said their vows and both meant every word.

Then the anvil was struck and they were husband and wife yet the fun had only just started.

Yes, it had all been planned.

A photographer was waiting and photos were taken outside the old blacksmith's and by the sign that said 'Gretna Green'. A little while later the first images came to Hugh's phone as they sat holding hands and trying to eat at the same time, with Emily's shoes on the floor beside her feet.

'Time to update our statuses,' Hugh said. 'Or do you want to ring your parents first?'

'Do it this way.'

Guess where we are?

He posted the image of them dressed for their wedding, kissing beside the Gretna Green sign, and not even a minute later her mum was on the phone.

Then her dad.

And then the 'likes' started and the comments.

What took you so long?

About time.

Congratulations.

We're all having a champagne for you both!

And a picture of colleagues and friends toasting them was posted from Louise's leaving do.

A cyber wedding party was happening and

it was possibly the only way Emily's complicated family could all be together to share in the celebration.

Her mum joined in, as did her dad and Cathy.

Donna got off the animosity horse and said she was thrilled and that the twins were really excited and would love to see them both soon.

'Wow!' Emily blinked.

Jonathan had clearly told Jennifer because she sent a long message saying she was ringing Alex with the happy news now.

Then came a message from Jessica.

Wonderful news. Mum says to say she is pleased for you. xx

It was very nice to know that Katrina perhaps had cared after all.

'I thought she'd forgotten me,' Emily admitted.

'No.' Hugh told her he had seen her in the recovery ward and how awkward Katrina had been. 'Sometimes people don't like to look at their mistakes. She was angry with your father, it was never about you.'

'I know.'

It was just nice to have it confirmed.

Yes, it was the best wedding, but just as Hugh went to switch off his phone and get back to the two of them, Emily took out hers and posted a little teaser of her own.

More good news to come.

There was.

Emily knew it and so did Hugh.

Finally she was safe in love.

* * * * *

MILLS & BOON®
Large Print Medical

June

MIDWIFE'S CHRISTMAS PROPOSAL	Fiona McArthur
MIDWIFE'S MISTLETOE BABY	Fiona McArthur
A BABY ON HER CHRISTMAS LIST	Louisa George
A FAMILY THIS CHRISTMAS	Sue MacKay
FALLING FOR DR DECEMBER	Susanne Hampton
SNOWBOUND WITH THE SURGEON	Annie Claydon

July

HOW TO FIND A MAN IN FIVE DATES	Tina Beckett
BREAKING HER NO-DATING RULE	Amalie Berlin
IT HAPPENED ONE NIGHT SHIFT	Amy Andrews
TAMED BY HER ARMY DOC'S TOUCH	Lucy Ryder
A CHILD TO BIND THEM	Lucy Clark
THE BABY THAT CHANGED HER LIFE	Louisa Heaton

August

A DATE WITH HER VALENTINE DOC	Melanie Milburne
IT HAPPENED IN PARIS...	Robin Gianna
THE SHEIKH DOCTOR'S BRIDE	Meredith Webber
TEMPTATION IN PARADISE	Joanna Neil
A BABY TO HEAL THEIR HEARTS	Kate Hardy
THE SURGEON'S BABY SECRET	Amber McKenzie